Brendan Buckley's Universe and Everything in It

Sundee T. Frazier

BRENDAN BUCKLEY'S UNIVERSE
AND EVERYTHING IN IT

Delacorte Press

Published by Delacorte Press
an imprint of Random House Children's Books
a division of Random House, Inc.
New York

www.randomhouse.com/kids

Educators and librarians, for a variety of teaching tools, visit us at
www.randomhouse.com/teachers

Library of Congress Cataloging-in-Publication Data

Frazier, Sundee Tucker.
  Brendan Buckley's universe and everything in it / Sundee Frazier.—1st ed.
    p. cm.
  Summary: Brendan Buckley, a biracial ten-year-old, applies his scientific problem-solving ability and newfound interest in rocks and minerals to connect with his white grandfather, the president of Puyallup Rock Club, and to learn why he and Brendan's mother are estranged.
  ISBN 978-0-385-73439-4 (trade ed.)—ISBN 978-0-38590445-2 (Gibraltar lib. ed.)
  [1. Grandfathers—Fiction. 2. Racially mixed people—Fiction. 3. Minerals—Collection and preservation—Fiction. 4. Rocks—Collection and preservation—Fiction. 5. Tae kwon do—Fiction. 6. Family life—Washington (State)—Fiction. 7. Puyallup (Wash.)—Fiction.] I. Title.
  PZ7.F8715Bre 2007
  [Fic]—dc22

                                                                    2006034041

The text of this book is set in12.5-point Goudy.
Printed in the United States of America
10 9 8 7 6 5 4 3 2
First Edition

To my grandparents
Vernon and Vera Strand
and
William and Willabell Tucker
For being there from the beginning . . .

CHAPTER 1

It was the first Sunday of summer break, and I was in a hurry to finish my dusting chores fast so I could call Khalfani to ride bikes. I wasn't even thinking too hard about anything, like Dad says I do sometimes.

Well, okay, maybe I was thinking a little bit hard. About Grampa Clem and how I'm going to miss fishing with him this summer. Which made me think about the funeral and how the man in the black robe had said, "From dust we come and to dust we shall return." And then I started looking more closely at the gray particles I was picking up with my dust rag, and I thought, *What is this stuff anyway? And where does it come from? And how come it keeps coming back no matter how many times I wipe it away?*

That's when the science part of me took over.

I stopped thinking about Khalfani and riding my

bike, and even Grampa Clem. And I definitely wasn't thinking about finishing any chore. I went straight to my computer and got on the Internet, where I typed in the search question "What is dust?"

Sixty-seven million, nine hundred thousand results came up.

I had no idea there would be so much out there about dust, but that's the thing about asking questions: They often lead to surprises, and they *always* lead to more questions.

I climbed our table to get a sample from the candelabra-thingy (it was the dustiest place I could think of in our house, since I never dust it), and went to my room. I set the microscope slide on my desk and pulled out the spiral notebook I keep between my bed and the wall.

Across the yellow cover, I had written in big black letters, CONFIDENTIAL. Dad taught me how to spell it. He's a police detective, so he knows all about confidential things. CONFIDENTIAL says that what's inside is important. Plus, you never know when you might discover something that really is top-secret.

I sat at my desk and flipped open the cover. The question notebook was my fifth-grade teacher's idea, but the name for the notebook was mine: *Brendan Buckley's Book of Big Questions About Life, the Universe and Everything in It.*

"Scientists," Mr. Hammond had said at the beginning of the school year, "ask questions."

That's when I knew: I am a scientist. Because as far

as I'm concerned, no question is unimportant, and nothing in the universe is too small to ask about.

I ran my hand across my book's title. Summer vacation had finally arrived. That meant seventy-nine days to find answers to the questions I'd already recorded. Seventy-nine days of scientific experimentation. And seventy-nine days to mess around with Khalfani, swim in his pool and get to the next level in Tae Kwon Do. Khal and I are only five ranks away from our black belts.

The thing I wouldn't be doing was fishing every Monday with Grampa Clem. When Grampa Clem died in April, it was sort of like having my leg taken away. You always expect it to be there, but then to one day wake up and find it gone? Suddenly everything's different and there's nothing you can do about it.

Now Gladys is my only grandparent, because my other grandma died right after I was born and I've never met my other grandpa. Mom doesn't talk to him. Or about him, either, which makes me wonder what happened. But I guess I can't miss someone I've never even known.

The one time I asked where he was, she bit on her lip, and her forehead bunched up like when she cut her thumb and had to get stitches. She just said, "Gone," and that we'd talk about it when I was older. So that's the One Thing I know not to ask questions about.

I turned to the front section of my notebook, which I'd titled *The Questions*. The back section was called *What I Found Out*. Under "Do centipedes really have 100 legs?",

"What's inside a black hole?" and "Do boys fart more than girls?" I wrote my latest questions about dust.

Mr. Hammond told us that scientists' questions compel them to find answers, and that's how they make their discoveries. I asked Mr. Hammond what being *compelled* meant, and when he said it meant to have an uncontrollable urge that won't be satisfied until you find what you're looking for, I knew exactly what he was talking about. I get compelled all the time.

I ran to the bathroom with an eyedropper from my microscope kit and suctioned some water from the faucet. I went back to my room, squeezed a couple of drops onto the slide and pressed another slide on top. I stuck the dust under the lens.

The cool thing about my scope is that it displays whatever it's looking at on my computer. I clicked a couple of times to open the program and up popped my dust—magnified four hundred times.

It was basically a bunch of small flakes. But flakes of what? I opened an Internet article called "Dust Creatures" and started reading.

The article said when you examine household dust under a microscope you can usually spot ant heads or other insect body parts. I had just clicked over to my microscope display to look for bug legs when a car door slammed outside.

I glanced out the window. Dad was back with my grandma, Gladys. A minute later the front door opened.

"I'm here!" Gladys shouted.

I got up to say hi because I wasn't seeing any bug parts, and because any minute Gladys would show up in my room anyhow. Gladys doesn't pay attention to my EXPERIMENT IN PROGRESS sign.

I stood at the top of the stairs that go down to the front door. Gladys was bent over, pulling off her shoes.

"These bad boys got to *go*!"

Dad tried to squeeze in behind her.

Gladys looked at him over her shoulder with her eyebrows raised. "Where's the fire?"

Mom says that Gladys can be *testy*, like a bull that's been prodded one too many times. Gladys's nostrils were flared. I could almost see the long horns coming out the sides of her head. Dad was about to get it.

"Hi, Gladys," I said. She stood up straight and Dad slipped past. He tipped his head at me. That was his way of saying "Thanks, son." Even if all my questioning and experimenting sometimes get on Dad's nerves, we're still partners.

"There's my grandbaby." Gladys started up the stairs. "Come give me some sugar."

Gladys pushed herself along by the handrail, as if she were a hundred years old or weighed five hundred pounds. She's old, but she's not crippled or hunchbacked or anything. And she's not fat. Gladys reminds me of a chicken with a rooster head. She's got skinny legs and bony elbows that stick out like wings. Her hair is short and black, but on top it's orange and piled up high like curly popcorn. It comes forward like it's going to tip over. The top is the part that makes me think of a rooster. And she wears pointy glasses.

I stepped down a few stairs and kissed her cheek. Gladys's cheek feels like a football. I know because I tried kissing a football once to see if it felt like Gladys's face. Gladys's skin is about the same color as a football, too. I wrote these things in one of my observation notebooks, and I for sure marked that one CONFIDENTIAL.

Gladys pulled my head into her bony chest. She smelled like she'd taken a bath in stinky flower perfume. I choked back a cough. She pecked my forehead with her lips. "How's my milk chocolate?"

Dad's the chocolate. Mom's the milk. That's how I became milk chocolate.

"Great," I said, stepping back. "It's summer break."

"So I hear." Gladys climbed the rest of the way and hobbled into the living room.

"Dinner's ready," Mom called from the kitchen. She pulled her famous extra-garlic garlic bread from the oven. The smell was so strong, my eyes started to water. I've even done an experiment with Mom's extra-garlic garlic bread. She says the basement hasn't smelled right since.

"The cooks are okay over there at Brighton Fields, but food loses something when it's made for a hundred fifty people. I don't care how good you are." Gladys sat at her chair in the dining room. "I've been looking forward to this meal all week."

We sat around the table, just like we did every Sunday night. I was in my chair near the kitchen door (or cutout rectangle, to be exact about it—there's no door). I plopped a pile of noodles onto my plate. I liked having dinner with Gladys. It was always entertaining. But I missed having Grampa Clem sitting by my side.

Mom had poured me some milk, and iced tea for her and Dad. Gladys raised her glass full of radioactive-looking yellowish green liquid. "To my daughter-in-law, because she's always got my Mountain Dew."

"Anything for you, Miss Gladys," Mom said, smiling.

Gladys sucked the pop through her straw. She made a face like she'd just tasted vomit. "Is this *diet?*"

"You know what the doctor said." Mom sipped her tea. The cubes clinked.

"That old fart doesn't know what he's talking about. Look at me." Gladys flexed one of her bony arms. "I'm still going strong." Flabby skin hung from her humerus like a turkey's neck. (We memorized the human skeleton in science this year.)

"Cutting back on sugar never hurt anyone," Mom said.

"I want the real deal. None of this artificial stuff."

Mom and Gladys were getting into one of their tussles, as Grampa Clem liked to call them. "I'll never be sugar free, Gladys," I said. "You can still get plenty from me."

Gladys scowled at her glass. "That's true," she muttered.

"How was your day, Mama?" Dad asked.

She grimaced. "Bernard from upstairs is after me again. I keep telling him Clem was my one and only, but the man's head is like a block of cement. He's just not getting my drift."

Grampa Clem had been my one and only, too. My one-and-only grandpa. I sprinkled cheddar on my spaghetti and watched it melt. The cheese's edges disappeared, and the orange goo ran down the spaghetti sauce like streams of lava. I swirled my fork in the center of my pasta volcano, watching the crater grow.

The melted cheese looked almost—what was that word Mr. Hammond had taught us? *Translucent:* letting some light through. Some minerals, like calcite—number three on the Mohs Scale of Mineral Hardness—are translucent. We had started to learn about rocks and minerals in fifth grade.

That was another thing I would do this summer—go exploring for rocks. I could even start my own collection.

"You should take him up on the offer," Mom said. "Get a free dinner out of the deal."

"Yeah, Mama, what could it hurt?"

"My nose, that's what. That man smells like cat. You know how I feel about cats. And he's got two of the critters. Lets them crawl all over him." Gladys shuddered.

"He's probably lonely," Mom said.

I stretched my fork into the air to see how high I could get it before the cheese strings broke.

"All I know is I'm glad tomorrow's my day with my grandson. I got to get away from that man." Gladys stabbed the small tomato in her salad. "We still on for tomorrow?"

I looked at her just as the cheese snapped. I shrugged. "Guess so."

"You're still on," Mom said. She gave me one of

those my-baby's-growing-up-too-fast looks. "My boo's first summer without a sitter."

I wanted to say I could have gone without one last summer. All the girl did was watch mushy soap operas while Khalfani and I played Yu-Gi-Oh! in my room.

"Hey," I said, chewing my bread, "did you know we're turning into dust every day?"

"Mouth, Brendan," Dad said, meaning I shouldn't be talking with my mouth full.

I swallowed. "Our skin is constantly flaking off and that's partly why there's so much dust in the world."

"I never knew," Mom said.

"Disgusting," Gladys said.

"Yeah, and there are these eight-legged creatures related to spiders and lobsters that feed on our dead skin cells, called dust mites." I took another bite.

"Hmmm," Mom said.

"I think I'm going to be sick," Gladys said.

Dad put down his fork and stared at me.

I decided not to add the part about the dust mites going to the bathroom all over our house and in our beds.

"You've got Tae Kwon Do tomorrow," Dad said. "Have you practiced your *hyung* for this week?"

"Yes, sir." Not as much as Master Rickman had told us to, but I had practiced.

I finished dinner quickly and asked to be excused. My seventy-nine days were counting down, and I had a lot of questions to answer.

CHAPTER 2

"Come on, Bren. I'm going to be late," Mom yelled from the hall.

I was busy researching a question that had come to me during dessert the night before: How do they get the ripple in fudge ripple ice cream?

Here is What I Found Out: They pour fifty gallons of fudge into a two-hundred-gallon vat of vanilla ice cream, and a machine stirs it around with a paddle the size of a Ping-Pong table.

"*Now, Brendan!*"

I grabbed some allowance money from the small tackle box under my bed and hustled to the garage.

I climbed into Mom's car, a red Kia Sportage. Mom says red is her favorite color because she has red hair, but technically, her hair's not red. It's dark orange and it looks lit up from the inside, like this amber I saw in a library book when I was doing a report on rocks for Mr. Hammond's class. Except the amber in the book had a big cockroach trapped inside it. I drew a picture of it for my report.

Mom backed the car out of the garage.

"Why do we have to go to the mall? I hate the mall." I pulled the seat belt over my shoulder.

"I'm sure Gladys will make it worth your while. Candy, pop—all the things I won't buy you."

Dad is the one who makes most of the rules in our house, except when it comes to food. That's Mom's department. Everything's got to be wheat or whole-grain. Wheat flour, wheat pasta, even wheat pizza crust. One of her favorite sayings is "If it's not brown, put it down."

"Gladys will spend the whole time in the water-massage machine, and I'll just be sitting there waiting for her."

Mom patted my leg. "Time with her grandson means a lot to her—especially now."

She meant especially now that Grampa Clem was gone. If this had been the summer before, I'd have been going fishing. Grampa Clem and I would ride the bus to the waterfront and cast our poles into the sound from the pier. We caught an average of 2.82 fish a week. That's thirty-one fish in eleven weeks. I learned how to do averages in Mr. Hammond's class.

I looked out the window and thought about one of my Biggest Questions: Where was Grampa Clem now?

———

A few minutes later, we pulled into Gladys's parking lot. The sign at the entrance read BRIGHTON FIELDS: LIFE IN FULL BLOOM, as if everyone who lived there were a flower. Gladys is not flowery (except sometimes her perfume). She's more like a rock, which is why I like her. I also like her because she tells the truth. Truth is what scientists are always searching for.

Gladys was waiting for us on a bench in front of her building.

"Be good for Gladys." Mom kissed me on the cheek. I wondered what kissing *my* cheek felt like. That would be pretty hard to test, but I could probably figure out a way.

Mom called out my window as I got out, "Thanks, Gladys!"

"Am I glad to see you," Gladys said as soon as I was out of the car. "Bernard knocked on my door this morning at seven-thirty." She flapped her hand at Mom as the car drove away. "Let's get this show on the road. I've got a hot date with a massage machine."

———

We took the bus. Gladys is on a first-name basis with the driver. When she's not hopping the bus to the Super

Mall, she's riding it to Muckleshoot, the casino down the street from the Super Mall.

As soon as we got inside the building, I saw the sign. MINERAL AND GEMSTONE EXHIBIT AND SALE. SPONSORED BY THE WASHINGTON AGATE AND MINERAL SOCIETY.

Rocks! This was perfect. If the society had meetings, I had seventy-eight days to attend. My summer plan to become a rock collector was about to get under way. "Can I go check that out?" I asked.

"Be my guest. I'll come get you when I'm done"—she raised one eyebrow and smiled slyly—"and we'll go over to Kandy Kingdom."

"Take your time," I yelled over my shoulder.

I jogged to a group of tables in a circle around the mall's fountain, inhaling the smell of Super Mall cinnamon rolls. I walked up to a lady's table first. All her stones had been made into jewelry—rings, bracelets, necklaces.

The lady wore a long, transparent crystal around her neck. The pointy end attached to the chain had been covered in silver so that it looked like it was wearing a hat. A purple stone had been fixed to the front of the crystal. She reached up and touched the necklace. "Do you like it?"

I nodded. "Is it quartz?" Mr. Hammond had taught us about quartz. The most common mineral in the Earth's crust. It came in many colors, but it was all the same thing.

"You know your stuff," she said.

"We learned about rocks in school this year—for science. It was pretty interesting."

"Maybe you'd like to come on a rock dig with us sometime. We go out a lot during the summer months."

"Really?"

"Sure. Let me introduce you to Ed. He's our club president."

Perfect.

The woman led me to a table where a man was bent over, straightening his rows of rocks—dozens and dozens of rocks, in every color imaginable. Each specimen rested on a puff of cotton in its own white box. Blue veins crisscrossed the tops of the man's hands like Dad's road map; brown spots made them look kind of dirty.

"Ed, this young man is interested in the rock club."

The man looked up. His orangish white hair was slicked back from his pink face. His hooked nose reminded me of a parrot's beak.

"What can I do you for?" he asked. The woman saw she had a customer and hurried to her table.

I turned to the man, not sure what to say.

"Are you interested in minerals?" he asked.

"I'm a scientist. I'm interested in just about everything."

"A scientist, eh? Important people, those scientists." He picked up one of his samples and held it out to me. "You might find this one particularly interesting, then." He set the rectangular crystal in my palm.

"What is it?"

"Calcite."

"But it's clear. The calcite I've seen was more like the color of your hair."

"That right?" He ran his hand through the wave above his forehead. "Well, color may be a mineral's easiest property to identify, but it can also be the most misleading." He laid a flyer for the mall exhibit on the table. "Set the calcite on one of those words on the paper."

I put it down. When I looked through the rock, the words split. It was like seeing double.

"Cool. How much is it?"

"Five bucks. It's pretty common stuff. But that one's special because of the double refraction. It'll be a nice addition to your collection."

I picked it up and looked through it at the man. It didn't make him split exactly, just made him blurry. "I don't have a collection—yet."

"Never too late to start. How old are you—eleven, twelve?"

I lowered the stone. "Ten, but I'll be eleven in August."

"Tall for your age, aren't you?"

"I guess. I take after my dad. Or so people tell me." I looked down the rows of boxes, taking in all his samples. "You've got a lot of rocks."

"Minerals," he said. "Been collecting 'em fifty years."

My eyes opened wide.

"Didn't start till I was fifteen. So see, if you start now, you'll have a jump on me." He turned his back and dug through a box for something.

"If you start what?" Gladys came up. The massage-machine line must have been too long.

"Gladys, look!" I held up the calcite. "I'm going to have my own collection!"

The man turned around with a green paper in his hand. It said PUYALLUP ROCK CLUB across the top. "Come to this if you want to meet some other collectors." He pointed to the bottom of the paper. "My name and number—"

Gladys gasped. Her jaw had gone limp and her tongue was hanging out.

The man looked up. His eyes moved back and forth a couple of times between us.

Gladys grabbed the flyer. She squawked like a startled hen. "Not interested." She plucked the rock from my hand and dropped it on the table. The piece of green paper fluttered to the ground.

She yanked on my arm, but I broke free and stooped to pick up the flyer. The man stood frozen, staring at us like one of the wax dummies I saw in Hollywood when we visited my cousins in Los Angeles.

Gladys grabbed my arm again and pulled me away. What was she doing?

"Ow. You're pinching me. What's going on?"

She kept moving forward, herky-jerky. "Your mama's gonna have a fit."

We walked around the fountain. The man was out of sight.

"Why did you say I wasn't interested? I am!" I wanted to run back and buy my calcite, but Gladys's grip was firm.

We kept walking, as fast as Gladys could walk, which was pretty fast. She huffed and muttered about how she couldn't believe it and what were the chances and Katherine was going to be beside herself.

At the next empty bench, Gladys finally stopped and dropped. She held her purse in her lap and pulled me onto the seat beside her. She breathed hard. "Holy Moses."

I slumped on the bench and looked back at the exhibit. The fountain sounded like static.

"Of course you were going to run into him at some point. But why with me? I've tried to stay out of it." She was still talking to herself.

I stared at her. Who was she talking about? I lifted the flyer and looked for the man's name. ED DEBOSE, CLUB PRESIDENT.

DeBose. That was Mom's name before she got married. That was my dead grandmother's last name.

I started putting it together. Could it really be? Why else would Gladys be acting so weird?

I suddenly felt like I'd swallowed a bunch of rocks.

That man was my grandpa. The grandpa I'd never met. The grandpa who was "gone."

CHAPTER 3

On Tuesday morning, Dad came into my room early to say goodbye before leaving for work. He said something about my *do bok*, then ruffled my hair and kissed my head. I went back to sleep. When I woke up again, I had the Jitters.

The Jitters is what happens before I know something, but after I realize I don't know it. Gladys says I get ants in my pants. I think of it as an electrical storm going off in my body.

When I get the Jitters, my stomach feels like it's full of fizzy root beer, and the top of my head and tips of my fingers go all tingly, and my eyes get all blinky, and if I'm eating something, my mouth starts to chew more quickly.

I try to control myself like Tae Kwon Do tenet number four says I should, but I can't help these things. They just happen. And they don't totally go away until I find some kind of answer to my question.

My Big Question today: Where had Ed DeBose been all these years? He wasn't gone at all. He was the president of a *local* rock club. So why had I never met him?

My stomach fizzed. A minitornado swirled inside me. I had spoken to my grandpa for the first time yesterday, and he hadn't even known who I was. Thinking of that stranger at the mall as Grandpa made my brain feel like it was short-circuiting.

I got out of bed. My *do bok* was lying on the closet floor, where I had thrown it the night before, after practice. I smoothed the pants against my leg, trying to get out the wrinkles. I hung up the jacket and strung my blue belt around the hanger.

Practice had gone only okay—it was a little sloppy because I kept thinking about Ed DeBose. I hadn't said anything to Khalfani because before class and after, Dad was right there, and when we're inside the *dojang*, we're not supposed to talk.

I pulled on a T-shirt and some shorts and went in search of Mom. She only works part-time, and today was one of her at-home days.

She sat at her desk scribbling in the checkbook. When she saw me, she held out an arm and squeezed me around the waist. "I was just thinking about when you were in kindergarten and the teacher said you were going to learn how to write checks. Remember?"

How could I forget? Mom loved bringing up that story—especially when she and Dad had friends over for dinner.

I rubbed my eyes, which were still blinky on account of the Jitters. "I thought it was sort of advanced for our age," I said, yawning. "But I was ready to try." Of course, the teacher meant making check*marks*, not filling out actual checks like my parents did. That was a major letdown.

Mom laughed. "What do you want to do today?"

"Can I go to Khalfani's?"

"Sure, if it's okay with his mom."

"It is. She said so last night." I sat on the spare bed, staring at the back of Mom's head. Ed's hair had obviously been orange like Mom's before it turned almost all white.

She made some more scribbles. My brain pulsed. My fingers tingled. I clasped my hands and took a breath. I felt like a beaker about to boil over. "Does Grandpa DeBose know about me?"

Her pen stopped moving. She sat frozen.

I was asking about the One Thing I knew I wasn't supposed to.

"He knows." She started writing again.

"Why don't you talk to him? What'd he do that's so bad?"

She put the pen down and twisted in the chair. "Where's all this coming from?"

I'd promised Gladys I wouldn't tell Mom about the mall, but nothing had been said about asking questions. I shrugged. "Just curious." Mom liked my curiosity . . . usually. "Will you at least tell me something about him?"

Her eyebrows pulled so close together, they almost touched. "You miss Grampa Clem, don't you?"

I nodded because it was true, even if it wasn't why I was asking about Grandpa DeBose. "What kind of job did he have?"

Her chest was turning pink. The color crept up around her neck. "He was a soil tester, for the State Department."

"What do they do?"

"Oh, I don't know. Test soil. Make sure it's safe for growing crops. Things like that."

"Are they scientists?"

"I don't know if they all are. I guess so." Her whole neck had gone pink. "Does that satisfy your curiosity for now?"

I blinked a few times. I still hadn't found out what I really wanted to know. Where was Ed DeBose when he wasn't at the Super Mall? "Can I see a picture of him?"

"Bren, you know my photos are a mess. I couldn't find one if I tried."

Mom was always saying she was going to organize her photos, along with categorizing her recipes, clearing closets and planting a vegetable garden out back—one day. But she never got around to it.

My palms itched. My scalp buzzed. I swallowed. Time to get straight to the point. "Where does he live?"

The pink moved all the way to her face. She was like a giant thermometer. A Momometer. She turned away. "I don't know."

"Could he still live in the same place where you grew up?"

"I suppose so." She gripped her pen again. Not like she was going to write. More like she planned to stab something.

"That's close to here, isn't it? Why can't we go see him?" I stood next to the desk.

Her eyes looked serious, but they sort of drooped, too. "He doesn't want to see us, Bren. He's made that perfectly clear."

My forehead tensed. Us? Why wouldn't he want to see *us*? I hadn't done anything wrong. I almost dropped the bomb that I *had* seen him, talked to him, even. But a promise was a promise, and I didn't want to get on Gladys's bad side.

I went to my room and opened my *Book of Big Questions*. My grandpa had been missing for ten years. My mom didn't want to talk about him. Now suddenly I'd discovered him, and he was a scientist, just like me. Who else was he? Where had he been? And why couldn't we talk about him?

I dated my journal and recorded my questions. Now I *had* to find the answers.

CHAPTER 4

I pedaled through our neighborhood, past Olympic View Park, where Khalfani and I go to race, or practice wheelies and do jumps on our bikes. Khal and I met at Tae Kwon Do, two years ago. Now he's like my brother.

I laid my bike in the rocks alongside the Joneses' driveway and rang the doorbell. Khalfani opened the door in less than three seconds. "What took you so long, man? We got stuff to do!"

"I got something for us to do, too." I reached for the folded green flyer in my back pocket.

He stopped me. "Not as good as what I got. Come on." He dashed upstairs.

I stood under the chandelier in the tall entryway and pulled off my shoes without untying them. No one wears shoes in this house. The carpet is white—or champagne, as Khalfani's stepmom calls it.

"Hi, Brendan," Mrs. Jones called from the family room.

"Hi, Brendan!" Dori yelled in her high-pitched voice. "Take off your shoes!" Dori's only four, but she thinks she rules the place. She once told a policeman who came to investigate a neighborhood break-in that even he had to take off his shoes before he could come in. Being around Khalfani's little sister makes me think it's not so bad being an only child.

"Hi!" I yelled back. I took the stairs two at a time and hurried to Khalfani's room at the end of the hall.

"Close the door," he said. He held some kind of contraption that he had clearly made himself. "Check it out." He smiled so big, his ears rose up on his perfectly round head. Connected to his skinny neck, Khalfani's shaved skull looks like a brown lightbulb.

"What is it?" He'd taken a three-pronged garden tool and duct-taped rubber hosing to the outside prongs. The opposite corners of a handkerchief were tied through holes he'd made in the ends of each hose. It looked kind of like a slingshot.

"A launcher!" He kneeled and jammed the tool's handle into a hole in a board lying on his floor. Then he sat behind the board, put one foot on either side to keep the device steady and pulled back on the handkerchief. I kept waiting for the hoses to slip off the prongs, but they held steady. He released. The tubes snapped and the handkerchief went limp.

"Do you think it'll work?" I asked.

"That's what we're about to find out. I waited for you, since you like to test things so much." He grinned. "Come on."

"Where are we going?"

"Just follow me." He put his finger over his puckered lips and tiptoed down the hall like the Grinch Who Stole Christmas. I walked behind him, hoping he wasn't about to get us in trouble, but knowing that he probably was.

He slipped into Dori's room and headed for the pile of dolls on her bed. "Grab a few," he whispered. I had a bad feeling about this.

With our hands full, we rushed back to his room. He dumped his load near the catapult. "Open the window," he whispered. He turned to shut the door.

I set the dolls on the floor, then looked outside. Mr. Jones had set up their pool for the summer. The super-blue water reminded me of Ed DeBose's round, stunned eyes as Gladys had snatched me away. I needed to tell Khalfani what had happened. Hopefully I wouldn't get sent home first.

I pushed up the window, then unlatched the screen and shoved it up, too. I knew what Khalfani planned to do, and when Khalfani planned to do something, it was no use trying to stop him. We would sink or swim together.

He already had the first doll loaded—a small, rubbery, brown-skinned baby. It was a good thing she didn't know where she was headed.

Khal pulled back on the catapult until it was stretched as far as it would go. "In five, four—"

I joined him. "Three, two, one. Blastoff!"

He released the launcher. The doll shot straight out the window and disappeared. Khalfani whooped.

I couldn't help myself. I smiled and then laughed, even though I knew this was going to mean trouble. Dori would have a fit, and when that happened, Mrs. Jones always went straight to Khalfani.

We slapped each other high five and ran to the window. The doll lay facedown on the cement patio, at least four feet short of the pool.

"Ooh, that had to hurt." Khalfani turned back to the pile of dolls. "Your turn." He handed me a floppy, skinny cloth doll with a huge head of curly hair. She wore a bright pink shirt and a short, fluorescent orange skirt. Her feet had been sewn to look like she was wearing purple leopard-skin boots.

Oh boy. With my luck, this was Dori's favorite doll.

I put the doll in the handkerchief and slowly pulled it back. I kept hearing Master Rickman's words from the night before about tenet number two of Tae Kwon Do:

yom chi. "Integrity means knowing the difference between right and wrong and choosing to do what's right." Integrity was our *dojang*'s focus for the month.

My hands shook. My arms were getting tired from holding the slingshot tight.

And I really wanted to see if I could make the doll hit the water. I released.

The doll snapped into the air and hit the glass, right above the opening. I held my breath as she tumbled toward the gaping hole, bounced off the sill and landed on the bedroom floor.

"You aimed too high. Try again." Khalfani grabbed the doll and shoved her at me.

I was having fun, but I didn't really want to get busted, and I had come here with a mission. Physics and the laws of trajectory had given me an out. "Wait. I need to tell you about something." I unfolded the green paper and showed it to him.

"Rock club. That's cool. But how's it more important than this?" He pointed to his contraption. "Catapults are all about science, man! You should know that."

I jabbed at Ed's name. "That's my grandpa."

"I thought your grandpa died."

"My other grandpa. The *white* one."

"Oh." He held the doll by her boots and swung her around. "So?"

"So, I never met him before. Until yesterday. At this rock show in the mall."

"How'd you know it was him?" He slumped on his bed and threw the doll on the floor.

"My grandma Gladys freaked out when she saw me talking to him. And his name. That's my grandpa's name."

"Why haven't you ever met him? Does he live around here?"

I sat at the end of the bed and put the flyer between us. "That's what I need to find out." He stared at me. "But I can't do it at my house. Too risky."

"Risky?" He crossed his arms and looked at me like I was being a chicken.

"I don't want my mom to catch me."

"Doesn't it seem kind of funny to you that you never met your grandpa? I mean, my grandpa lives all the way in New Jersey, but I've still met him."

"Yeah. It's strange. But my mom won't tell me what happened."

He picked up the paper. "You've got his number. Why don't you ask *him?*"

My chest tightened at the thought of talking to Ed DeBose. Before, he'd just been a guy at a rock show. Now he was the grandpa I'd never met. But Mom said he knew about me. How could he not want to see his own grandson? What did he think about me? *Did* he think about me?

I couldn't let Khalfani know I was too scared to call. Tae Kwon Do warriors never showed their fear. "I want to see where he lives first, do some investigative work, like my dad does when he's trying to solve a case."

"Okay, but only if I get to be the lieutenant." He sat up straight. "Lieutenant Khalfani Jones. I like the sound of that." Khalfani's name means "destined to lead"—and he knows it.

"Fine with me."

Khal sat in front of his computer. He went to a people search site and typed in "Ed DeBose."

I grabbed his arm. "Wait. I want to do it."

"You said I could be lieutenant."

"Lieutenants don't do unimportant tasks like this."

"Oh yeah." He saluted as I sat in the chair. "It's all yours—Detective."

I rolled my eyes, then hit Return.

In no more than two seconds, one result popped up.

"'Edwin DeBose,'" I read. "'Milton.' I see signs for Milton on the freeway all the time. How far is it?"

"I know how to find out." He scooted me out of the chair.

Mrs. Jones yelled from outside. "Khalfani Omar, what's Dori's baby doll doing on the ground directly below your room?"

I reached for the computer mouse. "Hurry up! We're about to get it!" Mrs. Jones didn't mess around when it came to punishment.

Khalfani whipped out his arm and blocked my body with a *sang dan mahk kee*. I backed away. He found a map site while yelling back that he didn't know any-thing about the doll.

"Then why is your window open?"

I shook Khal's arm to make him hurry.

He swatted at my hand. "You're messing me up." He typed in his and Ed DeBose's addresses and clicked on Send.

I swallowed. A map came up.

The grandpa I'd never met lived only eight miles away.

CHAPTER 5

I ran through the parking lot, ahead of Mom and Gladys. Khalfani stood inside the door, looking through the steamy glass. We always wait for each other to go into the *dojang*. (That's Korean for "studio.")

"Where you been? We're going to be late," he said. Usually he was the one coming in at the last second. I didn't have time to explain Gladys's denture malfunction, which had burned up about ten minutes at her apartment.

"Tomorrow," I said, huffing. "We're going to Milton."

"On our bikes?" His jaws worked a huge piece of blue gum.

"The bus." I pulled off my shoes and threw them in one of the cubbyholes against the wall. "I looked up the route."

Mom and Gladys came in.

"Got it?" I whispered.

"Can't wait," he said, too loud.

Mom came up behind us. "What can't you wait for this time?" Mom asked.

"Hi, Mrs. Buckley," he said.

Khalfani looked at me with big eyes.

I pushed him toward the entrance to the *dojang*. "Our next promotion test. Bye, Mom."

She looked at me out of the side of one eye, which she does when she's not sure if she should believe me, then lifted her hand in a small wave.

I stepped into the studio, sucked in my breath and bowed toward Master Rickman, once again becoming Brendan Buckley, Tae Kwon Do Warrior. I moved to my place on the mat and got in *choon bee ja seh*—the ready position.

Khalfani smacked his gum and Master Rickman gave him the eagle eye. Khal ran to the garbage can and spit it out. Gum's not allowed in the *dojang*, but Khal isn't the best at remembering rules.

"*Cha rut*," Master Rickman called out. Everyone stood at attention. "*Kuk ki ba ray*." We all bowed to the Korean flag hanging at the front of the room. "*Choon bee*." Ready. "Warming-up exercises. *Shi jak!*" Begin.

Master Rickman led us through our warm-ups.

"*Yup cha gi!*" he commanded. I kicked my leg high and to the side, the heel of my foot hitting my imaginary opponent's chest.

I made a fist and punched strongly to the front, pulling my other arm in tight by my hip.

In the mirror, Gladys and Mom watched me. Whenever Gladys came to my practice, she sat in a chair at the back. Every time I kicked or punched, she kicked out her foot or threw her fist, her forehead scrunched into a scowl. I tried to keep my eyes focused *shi sun ahp*—to the front—but it was hard not to notice. She lurched and jabbed as if defending herself from swooping bats. Or maybe she was imagining hitting that guy Bernard.

"*Ki hap!*" Master Rickman commanded.

We stood with our fists pointed down in front of us and yelled: "Ha!"

Then we did the *hyung,* or form, for each rank, up to whatever rank we were. Khal and I are fifth rank—blue belts with a purple stripe, which stands for "blue sky helps growing." We're beyond the seedling and sprouting stages, but not yet to the "growing nobly toward harvest" stage. That will come with the purple belt.

When we were done with our forms, Master Rickman put a board in the mount on the wall. He stood in side stance with his arms in a blocking position. He reminded us about proper kicking technique—foot flexed with the heel out front. His leg shot out and back so fast, I barely saw it touch the wood. The board snapped with a loud crack. Gladys hollered and muttered something about a heart attack.

Khalfani raised his hand. "When do we get to do that, *Sa Bum Nim*, sir? 'Cause I think I'm ready now."

I stifled a laugh so I wouldn't break tenet number four: *guk gi*. Self-control. A Tae Kwon Do warrior is in control of his body and mind—his actions and reactions—at all times.

"Your confidence is admirable, Mr. Jones. Actually, you will need to do the *kyepka* to be promoted to the next level."

"All right!" Khalfani said under his breath.

Khal and I are both *you gup ja*, which means we have colored belts, not black belts. When we get our black belts, we'll be *you dan ja*. When we heard about an eleven-year-old girl getting her first-degree black belt this spring, Khalfani got mad. Since then, he's been saying he's getting his this year. Khalfani turned eleven in May.

"Speaking of promotions," Master Rickman said to the class, "the next test is scheduled for July twenty-fifth, so make sure you're practicing every day if you would like to be eligible to take it."

I gave Khal a thumbs-up sign and we grinned at each other.

Together the class recited the five tenets of Tae Kwon Do—courtesy, integrity, perseverance, self-control and indomitable spirit—then bowed to Master Rickman. I started toward the door, but Master Rickman stopped me. "Do you want to test for your purple belt, Brendan?"

"Yes, sir. Khalfani and I want to be *you dan ja*."

"You know, purple stands for 'noble.' I'll start working with you and Khalfani on the boards next week. You'll be ready."

"Great!"

"Your dad will be proud."

I beamed thinking about Dad watching me break boards with my feet and receiving my noble purple belt.

He patted my back. I met Khalfani at the door. "He says we can be ready for purple," I said.

"Bring it on!" he said. "Black belts, here we come."

Mom and Gladys met us in the shoe room. I said goodbye to Khalfani, who left with his dad. I grabbed my shoes. "Mom, can we have pizza for dinner?"

"Sounds good to me!" Gladys said.

A little boy stood off to the side, watching us. "Mommy," he said. His mom was talking to another parent. He pulled on her pant leg, then pointed in my direction. "Why don't they match?"

I looked at my feet. Had I accidentally put on two different shoes?

The boy tugged on the woman again. "Why don't that boy and his mommy match?" He and his mom both had brown skin.

The woman stopped talking. She whispered something to the little boy about not being rude. The other lady took her daughter and left.

My muscles had tensed and my armpits were hot. Mom put her arm around me.

"What kind of fool question is that?" Gladys said loudly. "Sister, you need to teach your child that black people come in all shades." Mom let out a small laugh.

My face felt like it was a bright reddish brown shade right about then.

The woman glared at Gladys and beckoned for her older son to hurry up. She pushed her kids out the door.

"And teach him some manners while you're at it," Gladys muttered after they'd gone.

"You know, Miss Gladys, I'm not black," Mom said, laughing again.

"More Caucasian people got black in 'em than care to admit it."

On the way home, I thought about being black. I don't think about it all that much. Until something happens like that kid saying my mom and I don't match. Then I remember that my skin makes me stand out in some places—like with my mom.

Truthfully, I hear more about how tall I am or how good I am at science than anything about what race I am. But I know I'm black and I'm glad to be that, because that's what Grampa Clem was and what Dad and Gladys and Khalfani are.

If I ever wish something were different, maybe it's that Mom was black, too, or at least had brown skin like the rest of us. Then I wouldn't get asked about what I am all the time at school. Seems like things would be simpler.

And there'd be no question about whether we belong together.

CHAPTER 6

The next morning, I had breakfast with my parents. Mom made French toast, my favorite.

"I want you to call me at work today." Mom poured a small circle of syrup at the side of her French toast. "No forgetting like you did on Wednesday, or I'll send you to Gladys's."

"Now, there's a serious threat." Dad's eyes smiled, even though his mouth was busy chewing sausage.

"If I don't hear from you by noon, I'll be calling Mrs. Jones to make sure you're all right."

I'd have to find a phone, even though I didn't know exactly where I'd be. Somewhere in Milton. Tracking down my long-gone grandpa.

"Okay." I kept my chin down. I don't really believe in mental telepathy because it's not scientific, but I couldn't be too careful. I had this feeling that if Mom looked into my eyes she'd be able to tell where I planned to go today. I covered every square millimeter of my French toast with syrup.

"I heard what happened after Tae Kwon Do last night," Dad said. "With the little boy." He piled his French toast and cut it all at once so he could get four bites in one.

I shrugged. "He was just a curious kid," I said.

"You should know something about that." Dad shoved the toast tower into his mouth.

Mom spoke. "You know, sweetie, there are plenty of ways we do match, even if we're not the same color." She pushed her hair behind her ear. "We've both got freckles on our noses, for one," she said. "And green eyes . . ."

"And you've got the same great smile," Dad said with his mouth still full. Sometimes Dad forgets his own rules. He reached out and put his arm next to mine. "We're not exactly the same color, either, are we?" he asked.

"Black people come in all shades," I said, remembering Gladys's words.

"That's true," Dad said, pulling back his arm, "and the world *is* going to see you as black." He stabbed another stack of French toast bites. "You know how I feel about that."

Dad was always saying how I needed to learn to control my actions and most of all my anger, because people look at black boys more suspiciously than they look at others. I think he started me in Tae Kwon Do so I would learn how to stay cool under pressure. Tae Kwon Do warriors don't let anything throw them off.

He also told me that black boys get stopped by police more and are questioned more roughly, and that's why he became a policeman. So he could help change the system.

I don't understand totally. I've never seen people look at me more suspiciously. And I've never been stopped by any police. But what Dad says makes me wonder.

"You can also see yourself as biracial if you want," Mom said.

Black. Biracial. I guessed it was important to have a label, but I was still just Brendan Buckley.

I took my last bite. "Can I go to Khalfani's now?"

Mom glanced at Dad. "I can give you a ride," Dad said.

"I want to ride my bike."

"I won't argue with that," he said. "Gotta be in shape for your purple belt exam, right?"

"Sure," I said, but my mind had already left the room. I had a new question to write down, but this one didn't give me the Jitters. This question sat heavy in my gut like a big twisted knot that I had to figure out how to untie. Or maybe that was the French toast.

I went to my room and pulled out my *Book of Big*

Questions. I turned to the first section. "What am I?" I wrote. "Black? Biracial? Am I white, too?"

I shoved my question notebook into my backpack. I grabbed the *Official Rock Collectors' Field Guide* I'd checked out at the library the day before and looked at more of the pictures. I had gotten a stack of books on rocks and minerals so I could read up on the subject—because I was interested, but also in case I saw Ed DeBose again. If I knew some things about rocks, maybe he'd be impressed and want to hear what else I knew.

I put the field guide in my pack, said goodbye to Mom and Dad and took off.

————————

Riding my bike to Khalfani's, I went over the plan in my head. I had the bus numbers and times memorized. I knew where we needed to transfer and where to get off.

I pedaled slowly, my back and face heating up under the sun. I noticed how much around me was made of rock, just like one of the library books had said. The sidewalk, street, walls, driveways and a lot of stuff in houses and roofs—they wouldn't be here if it weren't for rocks and minerals. I crossed the stone footbridge at Olympic View Park, the water flowing over rocks in the creek bed below.

All the reading I'd done and pictures I'd seen the night before had given me more Big Questions. Like what made diamond the hardest mineral in the world? And how was it possible to pound an ounce of gold thin enough to cover a football field? And what made minerals come in so many different colors?

The field guide showed pictures of dozens of minerals. One had thin, needlelike, bright pink crystals and looked like a sea urchin. Another had orange-red, pointy, clumped crystals like flames that had turned to glistening rock. And there was one with blue crystals the color of Mom's toilet bowl cleaner, covered with copper-orange dust. I liked the polished chunk of hematite best. It looked like a silvery-black alien brain.

Different colors... just like people. I remembered again the little boy from the night before: "Why don't they match?"

Why different colors? Grampa Clem had once said that God made people different colors to test us—and we'd been failing ever since.

I stopped my bike at the railroad tracks and picked up a piece of solid black rock from between the ties. Basalt. I'd read about it in one of the library books. It was an igneous rock formed from magma that seeped up through cracks in the ground and got hard. Magma was underground lava. I shoved the rock in my front pocket.

When I got to Khalfani's, he told his stepmom we were going to the park, and we rode away on our bikes. This was all part of the plan. We would stash the bikes in some bushes near the bus stop and pick them up on the way back.

There weren't many people on the bus—just a lady

with her baby, a teenage boy and a few old people. I zipped my metro pass into my pack.

"Go to the back," Khalfani said from behind me.

I chose a seat about halfway down. "This is good," I said. I slid in, but Khalfani had to be difficult. He dropped into a seat three rows farther back on the other side.

I didn't care. Between Gladys and Grampa Clem, I've learned all the tricks of having a successful bus ride. Like don't sit near the front, because that's where the people with lots of bags sit and you always end up with stuff in your lap or spilled drink on your shoes. And don't sit in the rear, because you get all the fumes.

Besides that, Grampa Clem told me, black people used to have to sit in the back of buses because they were seen as second-class citizens, but then they fought back and did this thing called a boycott, and so now black people can sit anywhere they want to on a bus.

So the middle—that was the place to be.

After we made our transfer, I knew it wouldn't be long. My legs were starting to feel jumpy, like if I didn't run up and down the aisle, they were going to do it for me.

This time, Khalfani sat in the seat in front of me. He pointed out the window. A sign on a post read WELCOME TO MILTON, POPULATION 6,025.

The bus turned at an intersection with an Albertson's grocery store and a Dairy Queen on the corner.

I reached up and grabbed the cord to ring the buzzer.

Grampa Clem let me pull the cord, but Gladys always tried to beat me to it. I moved into the aisle. The bus lurched as the driver pulled up to the curb, and I almost fell into an old white man's lap. He glared.

"Sorry," I said.

As we walked down the street, I kept thinking about the man on the bus and how he had looked at me. What if Ed DeBose was actually a mean man? My intestines started to feel bubbly, like hot magma moving around below my stomach.

Did Ed DeBose really not want to have anything to do with my family? If that was true, what would he do when I showed up at his house?

I pushed the questions out of my mind and tried to remember what he looked like. His face had been pink, his hair orangish white, like calcite. Mostly I remembered his hands and how they had been straightening those little boxes of rocks. And he had been friendly. He had invited me to his club meeting.

But that was before Gladys showed up. She had known who he was. Had he figured out who we were? Thinking about talking to him put a lump in my throat the size of a piece of coal.

We passed Mr. Sudsy Car Wash, Surprise Lake Middle School and a skate park where boys in knit caps and no shirts zoomed back and forth on their skateboards. On a peak a few blocks away, a water tower rose up above everything else.

"You got the map?" I asked.

Khalfani pulled it out of his back pocket. This was also part of the plan. He had printed it at his house, just to be safe.

"He lives on Emerald Street," I said. "That's a mineral. Also known as beryl."

"Way ahead of you." He held up the paper. He'd highlighted the route with a yellow marker. "Don't forget who's the lieutenant here."

"Whatever you say." The sidewalks had disappeared. We walked along a gravel shoulder. The houses sat back from the road, with flowers growing in rectangles of dirt, and large grassy yards. They looked like one-story LEGO houses.

We hit Emerald Street. "Right," Khalfani ordered.

"Yes, sir." A car with a loose muffler came up behind us and my palms got sweaty as I wondered if it was Ed DeBose. Part of me hoped he wouldn't be home. The car rattled past. The driver was a lady with a big hairdo. I wiped my hands on my pants.

"Here it is," Khalfani said.

And there it was: 1425 Emerald Street. I stopped and stared. We stood in the street in plain sight, like two deer waiting to get shot.

The house was half one thing, half another—white siding above and brick below. It looked heavy on the bottom. Bright green turf, like on an artificial football field, covered the porch and the steps leading to the door. An American flag fluttered on a pole sticking out from the front of the house.

The roses stood straight—like if they got out of line, they'd lose their recess. The grass looked like Dad's hair after a trip to the barber, short and perfectly trimmed around the edges, which reminded me that I needed a haircut. My hair was getting bushy. If Grampa Clem had still been here, he'd have taken me to his barber.

Looking at this yard, this house, with everything perfect and in its place, I wanted to turn and run. This was a house I should have been to many times already, a yard I should have played in. Inside lived a man I should know. A man who if he didn't exist, I wouldn't exist.

A truck sat in the driveway to the left. It was the color of limes, sparkly clean, except the hood, which was dull green, like the olives Grampa Clem put in his tuna salad. A shell, like a camper, covered the back. The truck looked like a little house on wheels.

"What are we waiting for?" Khalfani asked.

"He's probably not home," I said.

"There's a truck here."

"It might not be his." The license plate said GEMXPRT. *Gem expert.* That sure sounded like the license plate of a rock club president. Maybe Khalfani hadn't noticed.

He nudged me toward the driveway.

I walked up between the truck and the yard. A white wooden fence stood beyond the truck. I was about to touch the olive-green hood when I saw a NO TRESPASS-ING sign on the gate. I pulled my hand back.

Khalfani pushed past me and strolled to the foot of the steps.

"What are you doing?" I whispered.

"Ringing the doorbell. You're too slow."

"Wait." I walked into the yard and stood in front of the rosebushes. I stretched my neck to look through the large living room window. The curtains were sort of see-through, like fog, but I couldn't tell if anyone was home. I needed to think of something to say.

Hi, I'm Brendan Buckley, your grandson. I couldn't just say it like that, could I?

Good afternoon, I'm Brendan, Katherine's son. No. Too formal.

Hey, Gramps, what's up? Too Khalfani.

Hello, sir. I'm Brendan, and I think we might be related. That sounded okay. I'd go with that.

"You want him to catch you spying on him?" Khalfani leaned on the black iron railing near the stairs.

"All right, all right." I tiptoed past him, up the steps, and stood in front of the door. Khal ran his hand across the bars of the railing, making a pinging noise. "Shhh." I put my finger to my lips.

My hand felt sweaty and shaky as I reached for the doorbell. A sticker on the screen door said NO SOLICITING. The lump in my throat grew to the size of a meteorite.

At the sound of the chime, a dog came bounding

from somewhere inside. I jumped. My heart pounded so hard, I thought if I looked down, I'd see my shirt moving.

The animal barked and scratched at the door.

"I hope your grandpa's nicer than his dog," Khalfani said.

I swallowed, trying to get the meteorite down.

The door opened a crack and the dog's head appeared behind the screen. It wasn't a big dog. Just medium. White with large brown patches that made it hard to tell if it was a white dog with brown spots or a brown dog with white spots.

A large hand, also covered with brown spots, grabbed the dog's collar. I remembered those hands. The dog strained forward, still barking. I felt like I was under a spell—I couldn't get myself to look up at the person at the other end of that hand. Khalfani poked me from behind.

"Uh, hello," I said. The rest of my prepared introduction wouldn't come out.

"Sorry, boys. Not today." His voice was rough, like unpolished granite.

I looked up just in time to see the door close.

I stared at the crisscross pattern of the screen until my eyes blurred. Didn't he even remember me from the other day?

"Was that him?" Khalfani asked.

I nodded.

"What'd he do that for?"

"I don't know."

"You're not going to let him shut the door in your face, are you?" Khalfani reached for the doorbell.

I grabbed his arm. "Wait." I pushed the bell. The chime rang again, but there was no more barking. Finally, the door opened.

"Look, kid, didn't you see the sign on my door? I'm not buying anything." The creases in his forehead ran in straight lines, like the grooves in Dad's old records.

"We're not selling anything," I said.

I looked into his pool-water blue eyes. Grampa Clem told me always to look into people's eyes. It was the only way to know the soul of a person, he said. The old man's eyes were the color of the mineral azurite, but duller. "I was at the mall," I said. "At the rock show."

Ed DeBose peered through the screen as if he was trying to recognize me. "The double-refracting calcite?"

I nodded.

"Yeah, I remember now. Where'd you go in such a hurry?"

What should I tell him? That my grandma dragged me off because she knew he was the grandpa we never talked about?

He pushed the door open. "Come inside."

CHAPTER 7

Ed DeBose's walls were as white and smooth as eggshells. I could practically see my reflection in the polished wood floors. Across the room hung a large framed picture of four people.

I stared at it, hard.

There, in front, smiled Mom. She had braces on her teeth, and her hair hung down past her shoulders, but it was Mom. A woman I guessed was Grandma DeBose sat next to her, and behind Grandma DeBose stood Mom's older brother, wearing a suit and tie.

The other person in the picture stood in front of me, just a little more pink and a lot more creased. Grandpa DeBose.

The dog sniffed my hand. "What's his name?" I asked, stroking his head.

"P.J.—Patches Junior."

"So there was a Patches Senior?"

"Had to put him down years back. Got rabies from a raccoon."

Mom had told me that story. It was why she never wanted to have another dog.

"Was that your grandma at the mall?"

I nodded. Had he recognized her? Did he know he was my grandpa? It sure didn't seem like it.

"What crazy bug crawled under her skin?"

I shrugged, then stared at the picture, frozen like a petrified tree trunk.

Ed DeBose looked in the direction of the portrait, then back at me. The skin between his eyes crinkled. "You must really want that calcite to track down where I live."

I nodded again.

He moved toward the wall and a display case on the left. He flipped a switch and the case glowed. It was full of amazing-looking rocks, just like the ones I'd seen in my library books. The specimens glistened in the light.

Khalfani elbowed me. "Aren't you going to tell him?" he whispered.

"Not yet," I mouthed back. If Khal opened his big mouth...I stepped closer to take a look. One rock in particular caught my attention. It sat in the center of the case under a spotlight—sliced in half and set on a stand so you could see the inside. It was perfectly blue, like the sky after rain. I thought I could even see a rain-bow running through it, like the surface of oil on a sunny day. "What is that one?" I asked, pointing.

I could see Ed's pink face in the glass. "Ellensburg Blue. Not for sale. Only agate considered a precious stone by the Smithsonian Institute."

Ellensburg Blue. I hadn't heard of that one before. I wondered how I could get some.

"Everyone argues about what color makes for the best grade. What I've got there is the highest quality you can get—as pure as I've ever seen." Ed DeBose opened a drawer under the display and ran his finger over several white-lidded boxes until he found what he wanted. "You're lucky I still got it." He opened the box and held it so we could see the mineral.

My heart thudded. My arms felt like they might drop from their sockets. "Do you know who I am?" My voice sounded like a squeak.

"I said I remembered you." He held it out for me. "You still want it, don't you?"

"Yes." I started to unzip my backpack for my wallet. Khalfani elbowed me again. I glared at him.

He glared back. "If you don't tell him, I will."

"What's going on here?" Ed asked.

I stared at the picture of Mom again. "That's"—I pointed at her—"my mom."

Ed's head swiveled on his neck, slowly, back and forth. He narrowed his eyes at the picture, then at me.

At me, then at the picture. "You mean to say...," he said, "you're..."

"Brendan, sir. Brendan Buckley." I couldn't get the words *your grandson* out, so I left it at that.

"Hmm." He rubbed his chin. "Well, I'll be a monkey's uncle. I thought that grandma of yours looked sorta familiar. Of course, it's been over ten years...."

Ed DeBose pulled on his ear. "How the heck did you find me?"

"The Internet, sir," I said.

Khalfani held up the printed map.

"I'm on the Internet?" Ed asked.

"Everyone's on the Internet," Khal said, as if Ed should have known this.

Ed dropped the calcite back in the box and closed it in the drawer. I guessed he didn't want me to have it now. I felt a twinge in my heart, as if it'd been pinched by tweezers.

The room suddenly seemed stuffy. I glanced toward the closed drawer. Ed cleared his throat.

"Do you have anything to drink?" Khalfani asked. I was glad, because my mouth was as dry as chalk.

"Got some of that instant lemonade," Ed said. "You drink that?" We nodded and followed him into the kitchen. The walls were as yellow as sulfur and the air smelled like bacon.

I watched Ed as he poured our drinks. His skin looked like it had spent a lot of time in the sun. His neck was as wrinkled as his forehead. Gladys said white people were always "worshiping the Sun God." White people, she said, looked up at the sun and thought, *Give me a tan, but don't make me black!* When I was little, I didn't know what that meant. I do now.

We sat at the table and drank our lemonade. Ed put a bowl of grapes in the center. He sat, popped in a grape and rolled it around his mouth, watching us closely, as if waiting for us to spill. He chomped on the grape. I heard the skin split and the seeds crunch between his teeth.

Khalfani gulped down the last of his lemonade and wiped his mouth with the back of his hand.

Ed looked straight at me. "So what's that mom of yours up to?"

I shrugged. "She works part-time—Monday, Wednesday, Friday. At a place for ladies who are having babies and need help."

"Sounds like your mom." He ran his hand up and down the sweaty sides of his glass.

"Brendan's dad is a cop," Khalfani said. "Mine's just a boring estate lawyer."

"That so?" Ed said to me.

"He's a detective, actually," I said.

"Been promoted, eh?"

"I guess." It sounded like Ed had already known what Dad did.

Ed stared at me. I felt like a bug under my own microscope. "Sorry about the ears," he said.

The skin on my face tingled. I touched my big ears. They stuck out a little from my squared-off head. Just like Ed DeBose's ears.

He opened his mouth to eat another grape. His small bottom teeth crowded together like barnacles on a rock. They looked real. Gladys's dentures stood tall and straight like soldiers at attention.

The basalt rock in my pocket dug into my hip. "I'd like to know more..." Ed's eyes narrowed. "About minerals, I mean." Flecks in the table shone like mica. I kept my eyes down. "Could you teach me?"

Finally, I looked up. Ed blinked a few times, then pushed back from the table and left the room. I sat for a moment, wondering if I should follow him. I grabbed my backpack from the floor. Khal scrambled to catch up.

Ed turned from the drawer in the display case with his fist extended. "Here." He dropped the piece of calcite into my palm. "For your collection," he said.

"You're giving it to me?"

"Sure."

"Thanks!" I squeezed it in my hand.

He gave me the box, then looked again at the wall and the family picture. "Katherine had a collection when she was a girl." He shoved his hands into his pockets. "Didn't last long, though. Minerals weren't interesting, she said. *People* were interesting." He turned back to us. "If you ask me, people are a pain in the neck. Way too complicated." He gazed at his collection. "Minerals, on the other hand..."

"Why do you keep talking about minerals? Aren't those just rocks?" Khalfani asked.

"They're totally different," I said. This was my chance to show Ed something I knew. "Minerals make up rocks. Rocks are a mixture of different minerals." When I'd read that the night before, it had made me think about the first time I got called mixed. I told Grampa Clem about it and he said, "Everyone's mixed with something, son. Don't you never feel shame 'bout who you are."

"I see you know some already," Ed said.

My insides felt light, full of helium.

"Minerals are pure substances," Ed continued. "They have a structure that can be summed up by a simple chemical formula. For example, quartz—" He opened his display case and reached for a specimen.

"S-i-oh-two!" I said. The soles of my feet buzzed.

"That's right." Ed held up a piece of rose quartz. I recognized it from the field guide.

I'd gotten two answers right already! I smiled so hard, I could see my cheeks.

Ed, however, wasn't smiling. He reached into his back pocket and pulled out a white rag, like a tiny security blanket, and wiped his forehead. "Of course I'd be *able* to teach you. And I'm sure you'd make a fine student."

The electrical storm went off in my body as I thought about the questions I already had for Ed. I unzipped my backpack to get my notebook.

"But what about your mother?" Ed's face turned so red, I thought if I touched him, my finger would sizzle.

I suddenly remembered I needed to call her—in less than fifteen minutes. "Maybe you could talk to her," I said.

"I'm not sure that's such a good idea." Beads of sweat popped out on Ed's face. He wiped his upper lip with the cloth.

The top of my head tingled. A twitch jiggled my eyelid. I had so many questions to ask—about more than just rocks—but I couldn't press him to answer them all right now. I didn't know how he would respond. This was my grandfather, but he was an unknown species to me. I took a deep breath. The electrical storm died. Things had suddenly turned gray and rainy.

Khalfani pulled on my arm. "We gotta go," he said. "My stepmom's going to start wondering where we are."

One final spark zapped my brain. "Do you have a pick I could borrow?" I'd read about this tool in the books. Every serious rock collector had a prospector's pick. And if I borrowed one from Ed, I'd have to bring it back.

Ed disappeared down the hallway and around a corner. His footsteps faded down a set of stairs. He came back with a black bundle in his hands. He unrolled it. In the center lay a pick, a chisel and a pair of goggles! The tools were a little rusty, but that just made them look like the real deal. He tied the bundle again and handed it to me. "Make sure you bring these back, now."

I thought maybe he looked at me like we shared a secret. "I'll be careful with them," I said. "Thanks. Thanks a lot."

As I passed him on the way out the door, I could smell his clothes. They smelled the same way ours did right after Mom did laundry.

Khalfani and I ran down the street. I held the roll in the crooks of my arms, close to my chest. I thought about where I would hide the things in my room so Mom wouldn't find them. Why didn't she like Ed DeBose? I just didn't get it. He didn't seem so bad.

At a gas station near the bus stop, I called Mom. Yes, I was fine. Okay, I'd be home by three. She asked me why there was so much car noise in the background. I told her we were out riding our bikes, which was true, or at least would be as soon as we got back to the bushes where we'd hidden them.

On the bus, I kept thinking about Mom and Ed DeBose. He was her dad. He didn't live that far from us. But they never saw each other. She never talked to him. And he'd never talked to us.

I didn't talk to my dad once for a night. I was mad at him for missing my baseball game, because I hit the winning run. But the next day he came into my room and told me about a little girl they had found drowned near the Narrows Bridge and said that was why he had missed my game. Then I felt bad for not talking to him. I hugged him the hardest I ever had.

Maybe Ed DeBose had done something like my dad missing my game, and Mom had gotten mad at him, but Ed never told her his good reason. It was a solid hypothesis. One thing I knew: Ed DeBose expected me to come back, and I would. For sure.

CHAPTER 8

"I gotta pee," Khalfani said, hopping from one foot to the other.

We were in my basement, supposedly practicing the *joong-gun* form for our current level. Whenever Khal and I get together to practice, it always turns into sparring. But *dare ee on*—sparring—is one of the four disciplines of Tae Kwon Do, along with forms (*hyungs*), self-defense (*hosinsul*) and the break test (*kyepka*), so we figure it should still count for something.

"You always have to go pee," I said, crouched in a horse stance. Even with my knees bent, I stood taller than Khal. Our height difference sometimes made sparring tough. Like when I would try to go for his chest and end up almost kicking his head.

"So? Everyone's got to go sometime."

"But you have to go more."

"Oh yeah?"

"Yeah."

He punched with his left fist. "Well, maybe I got a better metabolism than everyone else."

Khal *was* wiry—the kind of kid who could eat two hundred and fifty gallons of fudge ripple and still be just as skinny. I blocked him with my forearm. "Maybe you got a smaller bladder."

He punched with his right fist. "Who you saying got a smaller bladder?"

I blocked him with my other forearm. "You."

He put his arms down. "Well, you got a square head, Frankenstein." I was Frankenstein for Halloween this year. Mom painted my face green. I didn't need a mask because my head *is* kind of blocky.

"Well, you got a round one, Lightbulb."

"I don't got a smaller bladder." Kick.

"You could." Block. "Nothing to be ashamed of."

"I *don't* got a smaller bladder. And if you say it again, I'll pee on you." He raised his bent leg like a dog in front of a hydrant.

"That's not a Tae Kwon Do stance," I said.

He grinned.

Khal knew better than to do what he was threatening. I'd get him with my lethal *edan ap cha gee*—

jumping front kick. "I know how we could find out." My scalp had started to tingle as soon as I'd realized we were dancing around a question without an answer.

He put his hand on his hip and scrunched one eye at me. "Find out what?"

"How big your bladder is."

Khal's nostrils flared out like he thought I was a crazy man. I didn't let his look stop me, though.

I went through the door from the basement to the garage and pulled two pop bottles out of the recycling bin. Mom was at the store, so we could conduct our experiment without unnecessary questioning.

I handed an empty two-liter to Khalfani. "First, you've got to hold it as long as you can."

He shook the Mountain Dew bottle. "How's holding this going to tell you how big my bladder is?"

"No, hold your pee. You can't go until you think you're going to explode. If you go before then, we won't get an accurate measurement."

He looked at my bottle, then smiled at me. "You'll *never* out-pee me. I'm going to win."

Khalfani always turned everything into a competition, but I didn't care about that. I wanted answers.

We dropped the bottles and ran upstairs to drink water. We each gulped down a full juice pitcher, then Khal went for another one. After that, he ran around the house—into and out of every room, except for the bathroom, probably because it would have been too tempting.

I just stood in the living room and watched him jog around. He made faces as if he were pulling a train with his teeth.

After a while, I started to feel a burning sensation. I jumped up and down a few times in case that might help my bladder fill up faster or make more room or something. By this time, Khalfani was rolling around on the floor, clutching his stomach and moaning, "Ohhh...ohhh..." He beat the ground with his fists. "Ohhh...ohhh..."

Watching him flail like a fish, I started to laugh. I tried not to, because it made me have to go, but I couldn't help it. I laughed so hard, I peed a little in my pants. I limped to the kitchen and made myself drink another half pitcher.

I sat at the top of the stairs and pinched my legs together. I bounced my feet up and down. I cracked every one of my knuckles and both wrists. I leaned back on my elbows to make more room down there.

"Ohhh...ohhh..." *Pound. Pound.*

I could feel the pressure in my gut. The burning traveled all the way to my knees. I gritted my teeth and squeezed my legs together.

The garage door creaked and groaned. *Mom!* I tiptoed as fast as I could to the basement.

"Wait up!" Khalfani yelled.

We hid in the room where we'd been sparring. The door from the garage opened. "Bren, come help me with the groceries!" Mom called.

"Shoot," I whispered. I pinched my legs as tight as I could and waddled to the garage like a penguin.

Mom handed me a bag. "Where's Khalfani?" she asked.

"In the other room. Practicing some moves." I smiled, remembering Khal rolling around on the floor. Those were *some* moves.

I took the stairs carefully. One trip and I would lose control—and not of the bag of groceries.

Mom came into the kitchen behind me. "Do you know how those bottles ended up on the garage floor?" she asked, setting her bags on the counter.

I raised my eyebrows and shrugged, trying to look as uninvolved in anything having to do with two-liters as possible.

"Put them back in the bin for me, would you, sweetie?"

"Okay," I said, already halfway down the stairs.

I could feel liquid rising into my throat. My gut hurt so bad, I wondered if it was possible to fill your bladder to the point that it could actually burst.

I reached the bottom of the stairs. Khalfani exploded past me, screaming like someone running straight into enemy fire. I rushed into the garage behind him.

Khalfani didn't seem to care that the garage door

was open and anyone walking by would see him, zipper down, peeing into a Mountain Dew bottle. I pressed the garage door button, hoping Mom was too busy unloading groceries to investigate the yelling. The door rumbled closed.

"Ahhh..." Khalfani sighed. The inside of his bottle steamed up.

I pulled down my shorts and fumbled with the cap. Aiming into a hole the size of a quarter wasn't too easy, nor was controlling the pee that wanted to gush out of me like a flooded river bursting a dam, but somehow I got it to work. The quickly filling bottle warmed under my hands.

When I had squeezed out the last possible drop, I capped the bottle and set it next to Khalfani's.

"Ha!" he shouted. His bottle was half full. Mine was only about a third full.

"You drank more than me," I said. It was a variable I hadn't considered in setting up the experiment.

"That's not my fault. You should have drank more."

I didn't consider the results conclusive, but I was impressed with the initial findings. One liter for an eleven-year-old's bladder seemed pretty big to me.

"You know what this tells us, right?" I said. "You don't really need to go as often as you say you do."

"Maybe so." He straddled his bike and pushed the garage door button. "But I've also got a bigger bladder than you." He smiled. "Now let's go to the park like we said we were going to."

"First let's take these bottles and water my mom's flowers." I sloshed the liquid around the two-liter. That had been in my bladder. *Cool.*

Khalfani grinned big. I'd known he'd like my idea.

I enjoyed bouncing up the stairs without pain. I jogged to my room and dug out Ed's tools from where I'd hid them, in a box of winter clothes in my closet. I shoved the black bundle into my backpack and slung the bag over my shoulders.

On my way out, I let Mom know we were going to the park. Then Khalfani and I poured the results of our experiment into Mom's flowerbed and raced off, feeling a whole lot lighter.

———

At the park, we ditched our helmets and backpacks by a tree. Khalfani wanted to ride down the slide on his bike. While he wrestled the bike to the top of the playground fortress, I sat on mine and practiced balancing without the kickstand.

Khal rocked back and forth at the top of the slide, then flew over the edge, pedaling fast. At the bottom he caught air, just like a motocross racer doing a jump. His mouth opened in a big O. I watched, hoping to see a bug fly in.

His back wheel touched down. The front tire flipped up. Khalfani thudded to the ground and the bike crashed on top of him.

I jumped off my bike and ran over.

His eyes were squeezed shut. He moaned.

"Are you hurt?" I stooped, expecting to see blood. What if he'd broken his back?

His crescent moon smile appeared. "Got ya!" He pushed the bike off and rolled onto his side, but not very fast. "Was that awesome, or what?"

"Yeah, until the end. Khalfani, meet gravity. Gravity, Khalfani." I held out my hand and pulled him up.

"Your turn," he said.

"I've got a better idea. The stream."

Khalfani suddenly moved as if he hadn't just back-flopped onto a bunch of wood chips.

I ran to my helmet and pulled it on. I threw my pack over my shoulder. Khal just left his things where they were and took off. We always raced to the water. We zoomed over the footbridge—Khal almost hit an old lady—and skidded down the bank to the water's edge.

I dropped my pack and yanked off my shoes and socks. I would've beaten him, but a rock embankment at the base of the bridge caught my eye. Khalfani splashed into the water. "You're slower than a dial-up connection!" he yelled.

"Just a sec." I pulled the tools from my pack and took the prospector's pick and chisel over to the tan rock. Opposite from the pointy end of the pick was a blunt, square face that could be used to hammer against the chisel.

The rock face glistened with water and the slight green sheen of moss. I used the chisel and hammered away until a chunk came loose in my hand. I'd take it home and identify it with the field guide.

"Hurry up. My feet are turning to ice cubes." Khalfani stood shin-deep in the water, holding himself and shivering.

I set the tools and sample on top of my pack and ran into the stream, doing a spinning kick when I got near Khal. "Shower time!" I yelled.

"You want a piece of me?" He raised his hands and wiggled his fingers.

We kicked into the air around each other's heads and bodies, trying to make the other one lose balance and fall in. It was our usual contest when we got in the stream. This time, though, the bumpy rocks under my feet begged me to stop and look at them. Maybe pick a few up.

"Time out," I said, breathing hard. I put my hands on my knees and peered into the water.

"I'm just getting started!" Khalfani bounced around with his fists up. He jabbed a few times.

"Stand still. You're stirring up the water."

"What are you looking for? You don't wear contacts." He came over and looked down.

"Rocks." I reached in and pulled out a flat black stone with jagged edges. I was pretty sure I'd seen one like it in the field guide. Slate? I held it up, then dropped it into my pocket.

"Hey, kids, what're you doing? Trying to catch guppies for show-and-tell?"

Laughter. Older boys' voices.

I looked over my shoulder. Four white boys stood on the bank watching us. One of them picked up my bike and sat on it. White cords hung from his ears and disappeared under his Slim Shady T-shirt. His head bobbed in time to his music.

The tallest one stood with his arms crossed over his puffed-out chest. He wore a white tank top. "Or are you fishing with your hands, like the natives?"

"We're not fishing," Khalfani said through a clenched jaw.

My feet felt like frozen pieces of meat, but my face was burning hot.

A boy with shaggy blond hair spoke. "They're not going to catch anything in that nasty water except a foot fungus."

The tall boy smiled at him. "You know that from personal experience, Marty?"

The blond boy scowled.

The fourth boy, who had been standing to the side grinning, stepped up to the water. "I know how to make it nastier." He snorted long and hard and spit a huge loogie into the water. "Some seasoning for your fish!"

They all laughed then.

I stood still, not daring to move or to look away, but not knowing what to do, either. They were bigger than us. A lot bigger. And they had our bikes. But tenet number five told me I couldn't just jump out of the stream and run away. *Baekjul boolgool*. Indomitable spirit. A Tae Kwon Do warrior should never be dominated or have his spirit broken by another.

The boy who had spit glanced at the ground. "What's this?" he asked. My backpack. *The tools*. He grabbed the pick and held it up. "This looks dangerous. We better keep it so the little boys don't hurt themselves." He tossed it to the boy with shaggy hair.

I charged out of the stream. "Give it back!"

Shaggy-Hair Boy smiled and threw the pick to Tank Top Boy. "Monkey in the middle!" Shaggy called. He made chimp sounds and pushed out his ears. Was he making fun of my ears?

I rushed toward my pick, but the tall boy held it over his head. I jumped at it and bumped into him. He shoved me and I fell hard, wincing from the sharp rocks that stabbed my palms.

Khalfani blasted out of the water, yelling. He jump-kicked his foot straight into the guy's stomach.

Tank Top Boy grunted and stumbled. No one moved. The boy on my bike stopped bobbing. I'd turned to stone.

The boy regained his balance. He narrowed his eyes at Khal. He still held the pick overhead, but now he waved it in the air like a weapon.

I had to move. *Now*. I jumped up and stepped in front of Khalfani just as the pick came stabbing down.

High block!

My arm popped up, deflecting the force of the blow. A searing pain ripped through my forearm.

Tank Top Boy glared at me and raised the pick again. I forced myself not to flinch. I made my legs like cement and kept my fists near my face. My ragged breaths sounded like a steam engine. I could smell my sweat and almost taste the fresh blood oozing from my arm. Or was my tongue bleeding? It pulsed where I'd bitten it on my way to the ground.

The boy hurled the pick. I watched in disbelief as it spun through the air, hit a large rock and broke.

The tool lay silent, but I still heard in my head the clang of metal striking stone. The pointy end was gone. A jagged edge was all that was left.

"I think that's enough fun for one day," the boy said. He turned and climbed the bank. My bike thudded on the dirt as Music Boy followed.

I stepped toward the pick and reached for the handle with my cut arm. Spit Boy stood over me. "Hey!" he said to the others. "I thought *they* had purple blood." His voice sounded surprised, but it wasn't real surprise. He was still mocking us.

He stepped on the head of the pick and ground it into the dirt.

My forearm throbbed. Blood trickled from the gash. *Red* blood, same as everyone else's.

CHAPTER 9

By the time I got home, Dad's car was in the driveway. The lawn mower roared to life in the backyard. Cool. Dad was out back. I just had to get past Mom.

My arm had stopped stinging, but the rest of me was still burning up over how those boys had bullied us. Worse, Ed's pick was busted. I had found the pointy end and wrapped it with the tools. Question was, how would I fix it?

I snuck into the house and up the stairs. I tensed when I saw Gladys sitting on the couch—until her head bobbed and I heard her snore. Mom was nowhere in sight.

In my room, I took the black bundle from my bag and unrolled it. I laid the pick and its point on my bed. The tool's jagged edge taunted me like those rough boys and their sharp words. It was useless. The pick was broken. There was no way to fix it.

My chest tingled as I remembered the pick hurtling past my face and smashing to the ground. Why had the boy done that? Why had they even stopped to bother us at all? We weren't bothering them.

I pulled out my *Book of Big Questions*. "What makes people be mean?" I wrote. I didn't know if science could answer a question like this, but it probably could. Science could explain everything.

I went over what had happened, how it had started and what they had said to us. When I got to the last boy, the one who had stepped on the pick, my face turned warm. *I thought they had purple blood.*

Khalfani and I were the "they," and I knew why.

Because we were black.

For the first time I could remember, someone had been mean to me because of my color. I wrote on the next line: "What makes white people be mean to black people?"

Grampa Clem had told me about a few bad things white people had done to him, but it always seemed like a really long time ago. And there was Dad, with his warnings about how things were tougher for black boys. But it had never been something I worried about for myself. I closed the notebook and slipped it behind my bed.

I rolled up the tools and buried them in the box of

old clothes. I didn't even know when I would go back to Ed's. Maybe now I just wouldn't.

I took the chunk of rock I'd chipped off the embankment and the one from the stream and set them on my desk. I looked through the field guide for the picture of slate.

My river rock matched the description exactly. Slate could be black, gray, brownish red, bluish gray or greenish gray. Mine was black. The rock came in thin, smooth layers that could easily be split. I didn't want to split mine, but I could see the layers.

Slate had once been an easier-to-break rock called shale, but heat and pressure had turned it into something stronger, the book said. More than once, Grampa Clem had told me that black people had been made stronger by all the trials they had been through. That sounded just like metamorphic rock, I thought. I rubbed the slate between my fingers.

The rock reminded me of Grampa Clem. It was black and thin, not flashy, but solid. The rock's pointiness made me think of him, too. Whether he talked or you did, he wanted to get straight to the point. "You can be for Grandpa Clem," I whispered.

My stomach rumbled like Mount Saint Helens. Was Mom making dinner yet?

I went to the hall and looked at my parents' door. Closed. I walked to the living room. Gladys was reading her *Jet* magazine. She glanced at me, and without waiting for her to ask, I gave her some sugar.

"It's good to see you, too." She opened the magazine to the bikini lady they always put in the middle and clucked her teeth. "I remember those days," she said. I tried not to imagine Gladys in a bikini.

The door opened and Dad came in and saw me. "What have you been up to?" he asked.

A picture of those four boys on the riverbank—one of them on my bike—flashed before my eyes. "We went to the park."

Dad ruffled my hair. He smelled like cut grass and heat. "You guys practice your forms today?" He got a glass of water from the kitchen, then sat on the love seat kitty-corner from Gladys.

We had not only practiced, we'd gotten real live experience. "Yeah," I said.

Mom came down the hall. Her eyes went straight to my arm. She lifted it by my wrist. "What happened?"

I couldn't say anything about the pick. Then I'd have to explain where I'd gotten it. "Uh, Khal and I ran into some trouble." I sat next to Dad.

Mom's forehead wrinkled.

"What kind of trouble?" Dad asked.

"Kind of a fight," I said.

Gladys perked up. "You beat 'em good, right?"

Mom glared at her.

"There were four of them, and they were older. White boys."

"Oh, no, here we go," Gladys said.

Mom put her hand on my head. "Oh, Boo."

Dad sat up straight with his hands on his knees. "What did they do?"

"Mostly just made fun of us. We were looking for rocks in the water."

Mom inspected the gash again. "Then how'd you get cut?"

I had to think quickly. "I'd found a rock—a sharp rock—and left it on the shore. They started throwing it around and I tried to get it back and that's when it happened." That was basically the truth—with one minor change. "But I didn't run away," I said, glancing at Dad. "Because of tenet number five."

"I'm glad you didn't run away, son, but you have to be smart, too. If any of those boys had had weapons..."

They did, I thought, seeing the pick in the boy's hand. "One of them said something about black people having purple blood. Why would he say that?"

"Because he's an idiot," Gladys snapped.

"Just another way to say there's something wrong with us because our skin's a different color," Dad said.

"And one of the boys made monkey sounds at me," I said.

Dad sat back with his fist on his hip. His jaw bulged on one side. "Some white people like to think we're more closely related to monkeys and gorillas than they are."

"*Humph.*" Gladys crossed her arms. "Last time I saw an ape, it had thin lips and straight hair. Looked more like a Caucasian to me." She looked at Mom. "No offense."

"None taken," Mom said.

My most recent Big Question came into my mind. "Why are white people so mean to black people?"

"Some white people, honey," Mom said.

Dad spoke up. "It starts with the parents. They pass on their attitudes to their kids—"

Mom's head snapped to the side. "Not all kids," she said.

"I know, I know. You turned out all right." He smiled, but Mom had gotten as straight and stiff as the toothbrush I didn't use for a week when I wanted to see if I could grow algae on my teeth.

She patted my back. "Let's go, Bren. To the bathroom."

I held my arm over the sink while she poured hydrogen peroxide on the cut. I was so interested in how it foamed and bubbled that I barely noticed the sting.

Why had Mom ended the conversation like that? Was Dad saying that Grandma and Grandpa DeBose didn't like black people? Ed had been all right to Khalfani and me, so that wouldn't really make sense. Would it? Unless he'd changed.

Later, at dinner, Dad said, "You know who you are, right?"

"Brendan Buckley," I said.

"Brendan Samuel Buckley, grandson of Samuel Clemons Buckley. And you know what he would have told you?"

I shook my head.

"Don't let anyone tell you who you are, or what you can or can't be."

Gladys hummed in agreement. "And you ain't no monkey."

As I ate my chicken stir-fry, I wondered what my other grandpa would have told me if he'd been here.

CHAPTER 10

I lined up my growing collection on my windowsill—basalt, slate and sandstone, the piece I'd chipped off near the riverbank. I'd learned that sandstone was formed from hardened layers of sand and other small particles. Now I had one of each type of rock: igneous, metamorphic and sedimentary.

The only one I didn't put out was the calcite, my mineral from Ed. I kept that one in its box in the back of my desk. When I wanted to study it, I hung my EXPERIMENT IN PROGRESS sign on my door. Mom never bothered me when I had an experiment in progress.

On Wednesday and Thursday, I went over to Khal's, but by Friday I was itching to stay home and look at my rocks under the microscope.

I also wanted to work on some of the Big Questions

I'd come up with since learning more about rocks and minerals. Like why was malachite always green? And how could a rock—pumice—float? And was there any way I could get a real moon rock for my collection?

The answer to that question, I learned quickly, was a big fat *no*. Not without a billion dollars, and probably not even then. I couldn't find any for sale, not even on eBay. If I wanted to study moon rocks, I'd have to become a real geologist and get a job in an aerospace lab or a museum.

Sometime after breakfast and before I got hungry for the peanut butter and banana sandwich Mom had left me in the fridge, the phone rang. I ran to my parents' bedroom.

"Hello?"

Silence. "Uh, it's Ed DeBose here." He sounded like he had gravel in his throat.

Now it was my turn to be silent.

"Is your mom there?"

He wanted to speak to Mom? "She's at work."

"Good. I thought you said she worked Fridays."

"How'd you know our number?" I asked.

"There's this old-fangled thing called a phone book. I know it's not the Internet, but it works."

"Oh. Right."

Ed cleared his throat. "If you don't have plans, maybe you'd like to come to the rock club meeting with me tomorrow?"

"Really?" I looked at the photo of Mom hugging me on the beach in California. She kept it on her nightstand.

"You've got to be to my house by ten. Meeting starts at eleven."

Of course he couldn't come get me. "Sure." I'd have to figure out something to tell my parents.

"All right, then."

"All right."

"See you soon." He hung up.

Ed DeBose had called me! Hopefully when I saw him, he wouldn't ask about the tools. I rushed back to my desk and worked on memorizing the Mohs Scale of Mineral Hardness, knowing it might come in handy at the meeting.

The next day, I got up and packed my backpack. I wrapped my three rocks in newspaper so they wouldn't get chipped. I packed the field guide and my question notebook. The calcite went in the outer pocket.

I told my parents I was going to the park to look for more rocks. The fib just sprang out of me like water from a freshly drilled hole, but I decided it was okay. Ed was my grandpa, after all.

Mom's mouth bunched up. "You're going alone?" she asked.

I thought she was about to tell me no, but Dad

stepped in and said it'd be good for me, something about getting back in the saddle. So I got the okay.

I pedaled to the bus stop and ditched my bike in the bushes. I leaned against the pole and waited.

The whole way there, I thought about going to the meeting with Ed DeBose, the rock club president. I practiced what I would say if he asked me about the tools. I went over the Mohs hardness scale a few times, too.

At the back of my mind, chipping away on my brain like a prospector's pick, was a question: Would I find out something today that would help me understand why Ed hadn't talked to us all these years?

————

Standing on Ed's porch, my hands felt sweatier than last time.

The door opened suddenly. Ed pushed on the screen and looked both ways down the street. We stared at each other.

"Where's your dog?" I asked.

"In his pen. You ready to go?"

"To the rock club?"

"Let's go." He stepped forward.

"Isn't it kind of early?" I peered around him at the shelves of minerals.

"You can never be too early. You can only be too late."

We got in the green truck. It smelled funny, like a

bunch of mildew had curled up in the cushions to take a nap. Stuffing poked out of the seat in the space between us. The truck started with a roar.

"This is for you." He reached into the pocket on his shirt and pulled out a glassy yellow stone. "Corundum."

I held the translucent mineral in my palm. "Number nine on the Mohs Scale of Mineral Hardness," I said, hoping he'd notice I knew.

"Second-hardest mineral known to science. You know why it's so hard?"

I had no idea.

"Oxygen-aluminum bonds. Short and strong. The bonds pull the atoms close together. Pretty tough to break those suckers apart."

The way family should be, I thought. "Thanks," I said. I tapped it with my fingernail, then held it up and looked through it.

"Got that one there in Montana." Ed pulled on the lever near the steering wheel. We rolled down the driveway and into the street. He put the truck in drive and we took off.

"I read that being a geologist is like being a detective," I said. "They're both looking for clues to find out what happened in the past."

"I guess you could see it that way."

"I'm always trying to figure stuff out, too. I do a lot of experiments and write down my findings in a notebook."

"Experiments are the only way to know what's true," Ed said.

If I'd had a big lightbulb over my head, Ed's words would have been the switch.

Of course! Being with Ed was like doing an experiment! To find the truth about him, I just needed to apply the scientific method.

We'd learned the scientific method in Mr. Hammond's class: (1) Observe. (2) Create a hypothesis. (3) Predict what will happen if the hypothesis is correct. (4) Test. (5) Change your hypothesis if necessary and test again until you have a theory.

I had one hypothesis already: Ed had a good reason for whatever he'd done that made Mom mad. He'd just never told her what it was.

Mr. Hammond said the great advantage of the scientific method was that it was unprejudiced. Either something could be proven with evidence and facts, or it couldn't.

I rolled the window down halfway, then sat all the way back and let the wind blow across my face. I breathed deeply, smelling brown dirt and the not-so-good aroma of cows. I rubbed the corundum in my hand.

"What'd you do when you were a soil tester?" I asked.

"How'd you know about that? Your mom tell you?"

"Yeah."

"She talk about me, then?"

"Not really," I said. We were quiet. "I'm sure you had a good reason," I said. It was time to test my hypothesis—dig for some evidence.

"For what?" he asked.

"For not being around."

The skin on Ed's hands stretched so tight, the wrinkles disappeared. He cleared his throat and kept glancing in the rearview mirror as if he thought aliens might land behind us any second.

I started to wish I hadn't said anything. I thought about opening the glove compartment to see what Ed kept in his truck.

We turned at a white house with a red barn surrounded by miles of cornfields. Was the rock club meeting held at someone's house? Where were we?

Ed stopped the truck, moved the lever and pushed in the emergency brake. The engine rumbled. "You want to drive?"

My hands and feet tingled. "Really?" Khalfani had a race car video game but I had never, ever, driven a real car. Then I thought again. "What if I crash?" I always crashed the race car—an average of 5.7 times per race.

"My grandpa took me out in his truck when I was eleven. Taught me on a back road just like this."

I didn't tell him I wouldn't be eleven for another forty-three days. He got out and stood at the open door. "Slide on over."

I hesitated. Then I remembered Tae Kwon Do tenet

number three: *in nae*. Perseverance. Challenges help us to improve ourselves and therefore should not be avoided.

I zipped the corundum into my backpack and scooted behind the wheel. I *had* to—it was what a Tae Kwon Do warrior would do.

"When you pull this, the emergency brake will release, so you want to make sure your foot is on the brake, just to be safe. Which one's the brake?"

I started to move my foot.

"Point to it!"

I jerked my foot back. My armpits were as sweaty as a petri dish.

"I just want to make sure you got the right one."

I pointed to the pedal on the left.

"Good. Okay, put your foot on that one."

I pressed down on the pedal and gripped the steering wheel hard. Ed pulled on something and I heard a pop. "Don't move," he said. My body tensed. He walked around the front of the truck and got in on the other side.

My head felt light. I was holding my breath. I took a gulp of air. "What would happen if I took my foot off the brake?" I asked.

"Try it."

The truck just sat there. "Oh."

"Put your foot back on the brake and pull the lever down until it's on *D*."

I pulled the lever like I'd seen Ed do. My palms felt itchy. My back was sweaty. My face was hot. I sure could have used a root beer.

"Now move your foot to the gas, but don't give it too much. Just a light touch."

I felt like an astronaut preparing for blastoff. I picked up my foot and tapped the gas pedal. The truck lurched. Too fast. *Brake.*

Ed grabbed the dashboard. "Whoa! What'd you do that for?"

I felt stupid. I wished he would take over.

"You gotta keep your foot on the gas." His voice softened again. "Press it in a little and hold it there."

I moved my foot to the gas pedal and pushed down with my toes. The truck surged and I started to pull my foot back, but I remembered and held it still. The truck was going, and I was making it go! The steering wheel jiggled in my hands, trying to take over, but I held on. My arms vibrated and my teeth buzzed. It felt like someone was doing backflips in my stomach.

"Keep it steady. You don't even need to move the steering wheel. Just keep the tires where they are."

The road ran straight as far as I could see. We could go on like this forever. I was driving!

"How's it feel?" Ed asked.

"It's fun!"

"I remember being on that country road with my grandpa like it was yesterday."

Would I remember this day when I was as old as Ed DeBose? I was pretty sure I would.

We rode like that for a while, until my calf cramped and my foot felt glued to the pedal. I started to worry about how we would stop.

"Keep your hands right where they are. Just lift your foot." The truck slowed until a worm could have crawled faster. "Now, easy, place your foot on the brake and push it in slow. Real slow." Ed didn't even have to grab the dashboard.

"You did good," he said. His lips pulled down at the corners and he nodded his head. His jaw chewed on the memory of the past few minutes. "Real good."

From the top of my head to the soles of my feet, I buzzed. The only part of me I couldn't feel was my hands, which I thought might be permanently stuck to the steering wheel.

"Put it in park—*P*."

I raised the lever all the way up.

"Push in the parking brake—down on the floor." It creaked into place.

I looked out the back window, through the camper. I could see where we had turned onto the road. It wasn't that far, but it felt like I had driven for miles.

Ed DeBose had let me drive his truck. Just like his grandpa had done with him.

CHAPTER 11

Ed and I bounced down the highway toward the meeting. "Almost there," he said, which was a relief. I had to use the bathroom and I felt almost as ready to burst as the day Khalfani and I did the bladder experiment.

We passed a sign for the state fairground. "We go to the fair every year," I said. "My grandma, Gladys, always gets her picture taken with the pig. Not a real pig. It's just a guy in a pink costume with a big pig head and a red bandana around his neck." I talk faster when I have to pee.

"I know the one," Ed said.

"Last time we went, Gladys slapped the pig on its rear and said, 'Now go get some clothes on, you big hog!'"

Ed let out a big laugh, but I held mine in. I know

what happens when you have to pee and you laugh too hard. "I reminded her there was a real man inside, but she just said, 'I'm sure he doesn't mind.' I thought it was hard to tell since his smile was sewn on."

Ed chuckled. "Your grandma sounds like a real live wire."

"She is," I said, because I know what a live wire is like, and that's how Gladys is. Shocking.

We drove by the fairground entrance. "I always have my minerals at the fair," Ed said.

"How come I never saw you before?"

"Your mom probably avoided the area."

"She knew you were there?"

"Been there every year since she started high school."

I suddenly felt the opposite of laughing. All these years Mom had kept Ed hidden. She had lied. So if I hid the truth from her to see Ed, I was just making up for all the times she'd done it to me.

———

We drove up to a building with a sign that said PUYALLUP COMMUNITY CENTER. I ran to the bathroom and got there just in time.

When I came out, a girl and a man with the same color brown hair were coming in the front door. She carried a box labeled GEOLOGY KIT. On it was a picture of a bunch of rocks, a magnifying glass and a beaker of liquid.

I followed them into the main room. We sat at tables in a big square. Ed welcomed everyone to the meeting. I could feel the smile on my face. That was my grandpa, the president.

He gestured to a man he introduced as the secretary, and the woman who was the treasurer, and then he talked about some upcoming rock and mineral shows people might be interested in. I kept thinking he would introduce me, too, but when he didn't, I decided that was okay. After all, I didn't have an official position in the club. I was just a normal rock hound like everyone else there.

I looked at the girl with the geology kit. Her hands sat folded on top of her box. Did she come to every meeting? She was lucky if she did. She glanced at me and smiled. She had braces. I smiled back.

Ed introduced a man wearing glasses that made his eyes bug out like giant marbles. The man had gone on an expedition for something called thunder eggs. I sat up and leaned my elbows on the table, eager to know what a thunder egg was. With a name like that, it must be pretty fantastic. Did it rumble if you cracked it open?

He held one up. It didn't look like much—like a petrified baseball or a stone that might be hurled by a catapult. Its roundness got my attention, though. I'd never seen such a perfectly round rock—like a miniature gray moon. What made it so round? I wrote the question in my notebook.

He reached into his box and pulled out two pieces of rock. The outside was the same rough, gray material of the first thunder egg, but this thunder egg had been sawed in two. Inside, the solid stone looked like a four-pointed blue star surrounded by fire. *Wow,* I thought, *I need to get a thunder egg.*

The man passed the two halves around and while we all looked at the rocks, he told us the legend about where thunder eggs came from. American Indians said the rocks were eggs from the thunderbird and that thunder spirits who lived at the tops of the Cascade Mountains threw them at each other when they got angry.

The story made me think of Mom and Ed, two thunder spirits living on two different mountains. Were *they* angry? They didn't talk like they were. They just didn't talk.

After the man finished with his presentation, Ed said it was time for the rock swap and sale. People who wanted to display their rocks could do so. My heart fluttered. I didn't want to swap or sell any of my rocks, but I pulled them out to show. I lined them up on the table, including the calcite and my latest acquisition, corundum.

The room filled with chatter. I glanced at Ed, but he was busy talking to the thunder egg guy. I drummed my fingers on the table, then switched my rocks around so they went from biggest to smallest. No one was coming to see what I had.

The girl had laid out her specimens. She had a lot—at least twenty. She'd moved her chair so she was on the inside of the table facing out. I headed in her direction. Each rock sat behind a neatly handwritten label. FLUORITE, TALC, GYPSUM, SULFUR.

"I'm Morgan," she said, standing, "and these are my rock-forming minerals." She opened her hands, palms up, and waved them over the samples as if she were introducing trick-performing seals. "Display only," she said quickly.

"Mine, too," I said, but then wished I hadn't, because she turned and looked at where I'd been sitting. Mine didn't look nearly as good as hers. I hadn't even thought about making labels. "Can I pick them up?" I asked.

"Only if you tell me your name." She crossed her arms.

"Brendan," I said.

"Did you come by yourself?"

"I came with..." I didn't know what to call him. "I came with my grandpa." I pointed in his direction. "Ed."

"*He's* your grandpa?"

I started to get mad. If she was thinking we didn't match...

"You are so lucky!" Her braces practically blinded me. "The president is your grandpa! You must know so much about minerals."

My armpits got hot. "Yeah," I said, hoping she wouldn't start asking me questions about stuff I didn't know. I picked up the talc and rubbed it between my fingers. It felt smooth, like water. I looked at its silky surface under her plastic magnifying glass.

I scanned the rest of her minerals. "You've got hematite," I said, my voice rising in excitement. This was the one in the field guide I thought looked the coolest. It was much heavier than the talc.

"That kind's known as kidney ore," she said.

I could see why. It was rounded and bumpy like smooshed-together kidney beans.

"But you probably already knew that." She picked up a rectangular piece of white tile, marked with a few black and gray lines. "Have you done the streak test on hematite?"

I hadn't, but I knew what a streak test was from my library books. When you scraped a mineral sample against a tile, it left behind a thin line of powder. Each mineral had its own streak color, which sometimes differed from its outside color. The test gave more information about the mineral's identity.

She took the rock from my hand. "See what color it is?" she asked, flipping the hematite over.

It was kind of a blackish grayish silvery color. "Yeah."

"Watch this." She dragged the hematite down the tile. A dark red streak appeared. Bloodred. I ran my fingers along the scratchy scab on my forearm.

"Never judge a rock by its color," she said, smiling.

"The name hematite comes from a Greek word that means 'bloodlike.'"

"Cool," I said.

Ed called everyone together and I went back to my seat. "Does anyone have any questions before we end?"

I raised my hand. I wanted to ask about the thunder eggs.

Ed glanced past me. He didn't say anything.

I stretched my arm higher.

He looked around the room again, chewing his bottom lip. Finally his gaze came back to me. "Everyone, this is... Brendan." He said my name as if he wasn't sure it would sound right coming out of his mouth. "He found us at the mall exhibit." He talked as if he didn't know who I was.

The floor suddenly slanted and I thought I might slip from my chair. How could I be just someone he'd met at the mall? Why hadn't he said anything about me being his grandson? My face tingled. I was a rock sitting out for everyone to see. I wanted to be hidden in the ground.

My teeth bit into my bottom lip. My heart pounded in my palms. I rubbed on the scab again.

"You had a question?" Ed said.

I couldn't remember what it was. Morgan's stare bored a hole into me. She probably thought I had made up that Ed was my grandpa. "I forgot," I mumbled.

"Maybe next time," he said.

I didn't know if I wanted there to be a next time if he didn't even want people to know who I really was.

In the truck, Ed asked me if I'd liked the meeting. I said I had, and that was all.

We pulled up at my bus stop. Before I got out, he opened the glove compartment and lifted out a velvety green package. He handed it to me. "Take this."

I didn't know if I wanted any more of Ed's things after what he'd said at the meeting—or not said.

He shook it at me. "Take it," he said again.

I reached for it.

"You need a good glass to identify the minerals in your rocks."

I unwrapped it, slowly. A silver rim gleamed around the large magnifying lens—real glass, not small and plastic like the one in Morgan's geology kit. "Wow," I said.

"Bring that with you next time. We'll look at some of mine."

Would there be a next time? I got out, mumbled thanks and closed the door.

The truck coughed, then chugged up the street.

I held the glass to my eye, feeling like a detective still in search of the truth.

CHAPTER 12

I stepped off the bus, inhaling fumes, and headed for the bushes. I pushed aside the branches. My heart dropped into my stomach. I spun around. Had I gotten off at the wrong stop?

My bike was gone.

I couldn't breathe. My heart bounced around like a heated molecule. I flung branches everywhere, searching for a glimpse of the blue metallic frame. I collapsed in the dirt and crawled farther in.

What would I tell my parents? Dad was always lecturing me to be careful—people called the station reporting stolen bikes all the time.

I hid in the bushes with my knees pulled into my chest, breathing the rotten egg smell of the paper mill and feeling sweat drops trickle down the sides of my face.

———————

An hour later, I trudged up the front steps of my house. My legs felt as heavy and shaky as if I'd just spent eight hours at the *dojang* breaking boards.

My cheeks were tight where the tear tracks had dried. My eyes felt like jelly-donut filling. I had told myself a hundred times not to cry while I sat there, hoping whoever took my bike was on a joyride and would bring it back any second. But the farther the sun traveled in the sky, the faster the hope leaked out of me, like air from a punctured tire. I'd put my forehead on my arms and bawled like a baby.

When the sun had gone way past the high noon mark, I knew I had to face the facts. I'd done something dumb. I should never have left my bike. And now I would have to listen to Dad tell me the exact same thing, probably ten-to-the-third-power times.

The TV was on in the basement. I closed the front door quietly and moved quickly up the stairs and along the hall. Mom came out of her bedroom. "How'd it go?" she asked.

"Good," I said, keeping my eyes down and trying to sound like everything was great.

She pushed up my backpack from the bottom. "Doesn't feel like you found much."

"I don't want to pick up just any old rocks," I said.

She nodded. "Of course," she said. "Good idea."

I started toward my room.

"I've got something for you." She went into her room, then appeared again with a photo. It was Ed DeBose. He had his arm around Grandma DeBose and they were standing in front of their house. They looked a little older than they did in the family picture on his wall.

"I finally cleaned out my photos, and you had asked to see one," she said. "I decided it couldn't hurt." She squeezed me with one arm and kissed my forehead.

The truth scaled my throat and pushed into my mouth, but I pressed my lips tight. I couldn't tell her now. Couldn't tell her I'd been to this house *today*, seen Ed in person, driven his truck, gone to his rock club— where he hadn't told anyone I was his grandson.

But what about my bike? They would notice eventually.

I'd figure it out later. Now I just wanted to lie down. "Thanks." I looked at Ed again with his calcite hair and sticking-out ears and his grin that reminded me of another grin I'd seen in pictures.

Mine.

———

I stayed in my room the rest of the day with my EXPERIMENT IN PROGRESS sign on the door. When I had to go out, I tiptoed around as if the ground were covered with glass.

My promotion test was only a few weeks away and I wasn't prepared. In my room I went through all my *hyungs*. My first opponent was the tall boy at the stream. Then I imagined I was fighting the mystery enemy who had taken my bike. Sometimes when I punched or kicked, I saw Ed DeBose standing opposite me. Sometimes I saw myself.

When I came out for dinner, Dad patted me on the back. "Heard you practicing in there."

All through dinner, I waited for one of them to bring up my bike. No matter how much I chewed my pork chop, the pieces felt like they were getting stuck in my throat. Dad had been in the garage earlier. Hadn't he noticed the bike wasn't there?

Keeping down the truth felt like trying to hold Khalfani's basketball underwater in his pool. "My bike got stolen," I blurted out.

"What?" Mom said. "When did this happen? At the park again? Why didn't you tell us?"

Dad set his elbows on the table with his fist in his hand.

I kept my eyes on my mashed potatoes. "It was my fault. I left it while I went...looking." Again, not the whole truth, but not a lie, either. *Yom chi*, integrity, meant being honest. Was I being honest enough?

"I guess you better get used to walking to Khalfani's,"

Dad said. "I'll list it at the station as missing. Maybe it'll turn up."

"Yes, sir," I said. And that was the end of that.

―――――――

On Monday, Mom drove me to Gladys's. After the trouble I'd been getting in, she didn't want me staying by myself or going to the park—at least for the next week.

I said goodbye and got out of the car. I was glad Mom hadn't made me walk. It took only thirty steps to get to the front entrance and already my armpits were sticky. I sniffed under one arm to make sure my new deodorant was kicking in.

Dad had given me the deodorant the night before. "This'll help you with the girls," he'd said. He tossed it to me while I sat at my microscope looking at a dead fly I'd found on the windowsill when I was putting my rocks back. I didn't really care about girls, but I liked that I was getting to do something my dad and other grown men did.

I stepped into the air-conditioned lobby, feeling my sweat cool.

Nancy, the lady at the front desk, smiled at me. "Hey, Brendan."

Gladys said Nancy had a tattoo of an eagle on her back. It felt funny, knowing about the eagle. I would have liked to see it, though.

"Your grandma's at chair-obics. Downstairs in the rec room. She told me to send you down as soon as you got here." She held out the pen for the guest registry. Her long, curled fingernails were painted sparkly red. They looked like claws.

"Thanks," I said. I wrote my name.

I took the stairs to the bottom floor. A woman's voice boomed. "And lift. And lower. Lift. And ho-o-o-ld."

I peeked around the open door. About twelve old women and an old man sat in chairs with one leg stuck straight out in the air. Bobbi, the lady who led the building's activities, sat in a chair facing them. A lot of space separated Bobbi from the front row of chair exercisers. I knew why. Gladys said Bobbi was a real riot, but she had bad breath.

I scanned the room for Gladys. She stood off to the side, leaning over a chair doing her own stretches.

Bobbi was heavy on top, but she had narrow hips and skinny legs. Sort of like a buffalo. I've always wondered how buffaloes don't tip over, with such huge heads and tiny behinds. I'd have to write that one down in my *Book of Big Questions*.

"Now raise your right arm. And down. And up..." Her voice went up on the word *up* and down on the word *down*.

When Bobbi switched to the other arm, she waved at me. Everyone turned in their chairs and looked to where she'd waved. My face heated up like a nuclear reactor and I would have stepped back into the hall and waited until they were done, except that Bobbi said, "Don't be shy, Brendan. Grab a chair!"

I sat on the floor against the wall. Gladys continued her stretching as if she hadn't seen me.

At the end, Bobbi slapped her thighs. "Okay, folks, at one o'clock we've got the Melody Makers coming in to sing, so don't miss it. Come right back here after lunch."

"Are they like the Blues Brothers?" the man asked.

"Something like that," Bobbi said, "except they're nuns and they don't wear dark shades."

On her way out, Bobbi stopped at the door. She stooped and put her mouth near my ear. "Good to see you again, Brendan." Her breath smelled like an experiment we'd done in Mr. Hammond's class involving battery acid. "Don't let your grandma fool you. She needs the company. She still misses your grandpa a whole lot." She patted my shoulder and walked out of the room.

Gladys finally came over, dabbing her forehead with one of her ratty green towels. "What was *she* whispering about?"

"Something about candy in her office if I want to come get some." It was just a small fib, to protect Gladys. It didn't really count as breaking *yom chi*.

"Humph. She needs to get some breath mints in her office. Let's go. I need my Gatorade."

Gladys's place was stuffed like a suitcase, but not much of it would actually be useful to have on a trip. Gladys loved to shop at the Dollar Store. Towers of photograph albums, magazines and fifty-cent videos teetered around the room. A whole bookcase was devoted to shot glasses. She had more than a hundred.

I tilted back in Grampa's black leather armchair while Gladys stood in the little kitchen, opening and shutting cupboards. If I concentrated hard, I could still smell a little bit of Grampa Clem when I sat here—a mix of his aftershave and hair grease.

I gazed over the TV at the cartoon drawings of Grampa Clem, Gladys and me that we'd gotten at the circus. In my picture, I rode on the back of a tiny elephant. Our heads were blown up much bigger than our bodies, which made mine look even blockier than usual. If only I could talk to Grampa Clem again, I'd ask *him* about Ed DeBose.

A can popped open and the smell of fish times one hundred reached my nose.

"Want some sardines and crackers?"

"Gross," I said.

"Don't put down my midmorning snack just because you don't want any." I guessed nine o'clock was midmorning for Gladys, since she got up around five every day.

She sat carefully in the recliner next to me, the plate of sardines in one hand, her Gatorade in the other. "Uh-oh. I'm seeing the Brown Ridge Mountains." Gladys says my forehead bunches up like mountains when I'm thinking. She picked up the remote from the little table between us and turned on the TV. Gladys never misses *The Price Is Right.* "What is it this time?"

I shrugged. "Do you have any Ho Hos?"

"It's only nine in the morning." She set her food down and pushed herself out of the chair. "Just don't tell your mama."

"Like she won't tell me about Ed DeBose?" A woman was going crazy on TV, jumping up and down and screaming. Bells went off in the background.

Gladys glared at me. "I thought we had a deal."

"I haven't said anything."

"Good. Don't scare me like that, boy!" She brought the Ho Ho on a plate. "I got a new neighbor this weekend and I can tell already—she's one of those hysterical types," she said, nodding toward the TV.

I bit into the chocolate log and licked the white stuff out with my tongue. It seemed like maybe Gladys was trying to change the subject.

"Got a wiener dog named Dixie."

"A wiener dog?" I looked at her.

"You know—one of those short, squatty dogs that looks like a wiener."

Gladys had taken off her shoes and socks. I stared at her toes, pinched tightly together and slightly curved like little wieners in a sardine can. She put the chair back and crossed one foot over the other. "I went over there the other day, to be friendly, you know, and this woman had newspapers lying everywhere. She makes the dog do its business on the papers. She won't let it go outside to do regular dog things. I told her, 'A dog has outdoor needs. It needs to sniff around and dig in the dirt.'

" 'Oh, no!' she said. 'Dixie's too dainty for that!' It's disgusting, really. Absolutely shameful. That poor dog." Gladys shook her head. She looked very disgusted.

I held my nose because *I* was disgusted by the smell of that fish. It was making my Ho Ho taste funny. I set the plate down. "Why can't we talk about my other grandpa?"

She chewed on a sardine cracker, her forehead a big crease.

"What'd he do that's so bad?" I wanted to tell Gladys about the rock club and see what she thought about Ed not saying anything to people about me, but if I told her what I'd been up to, she could be seen as an accomplice. Dad had told me what an accomplice was. Accomplices could get in as much trouble as the actual committers of a crime.

Not that I was committing a crime. I just wanted to know the truth.

She followed the last bite of sardine with a gulp of Gatorade, then opened a small canister and pulled out a toothpick. She stuck it into her mouth. Gladys likes to gnaw on toothpicks, especially when she's thinking. She never actually picks at her teeth, because they aren't real. Once when I stayed overnight, I saw her and Grampa Clem's dentures sitting in two glasses of water on the bathroom counter. That night I dreamed I was being chased by giant teeth and gums.

Gladys picked up the remote and clicked off the TV. "You should talk to your mother about this."

"I tried. She won't tell me anything."

"I'm sure she has her reasons."

Why wouldn't anyone tell me what the reasons were?

Gladys squinted at me through her pointy glasses. "They had a big falling-out. That's all I can say." She crossed her arms.

"But I already knew that."

"Well, what more is there to know? Apparently, the man is as stubborn as a mule. Won't apologize for what he did." She reached for her crossword puzzle magazine and a pen. "Must be where your mama got it from."

"Got what?"

"Her willfulness."

I sat on the edge of the chair. "But what did he *do*?"

She slapped the magazine shut. "Cut off all contact. Wouldn't even let your mama see her own mother."

I hadn't known that.

"Then your grandma up and died. Totally unexpected." I'd never thought about how she'd died. She was just dead. "It's pretty clear your mama's never forgiven him."

"How'd she die?"

"Stroke, I think."

"You mean from too much sun?" Mom was always telling me to drink water when I went out on my bike so I wouldn't get heatstroke.

"More serious than that. Like having a heart attack in your head." Grampa Clem had died of a heart attack.

"But why wouldn't he let her see her mom?"

Gladys pushed in her footrest and stood up. "That's all I can say." Her lips clamped together so tightly, her upper lip disappeared.

I followed her to the kitchen with my plate.

She put her arm around me. "Don't you worry yourself about it, my beautiful brown boy. What's done is done." That was what Grampa Clem had called me—his beautiful brown boy.

I put my plate down. Over the sink hung a plaque that read "God grant me the serenity to accept the things I cannot change, the courage to change the things I can, and the wisdom to know the difference."

I'd seen that plaque every time I came over to spend time with my grandparents, but this time I thought about the words and what they might mean. I didn't know why I would need serenity to accept some things, or even what serenity was, exactly, but I knew one thing: I couldn't change Gladys's mind. She'd locked up the subject and swallowed the key.

I'd have to figure out the rest some other way.

CHAPTER 13

The reception area at Mom's work looked about as exciting as a prison cell. Mom had made me come with her today. She still didn't want me by myself.

A toy box was shoved into one corner. In front of it stood a short table surrounded by small chairs. I tossed my backpack onto one of the couches and looked into the box, just in case they had anything good. Mom had gone into her office and Denise, the lady behind the counter, was talking on the phone.

I dug through the toys, but, as I'd suspected, it was all baby stuff: some blocks, two Barbies—one brown and one white—a dump truck, little cups and saucers and a bunch of plastic food—pretend canned vegetables, broccoli, a banana and a pork chop. The best thing they had was a barrel of monkeys. I pulled open the barrel and dumped the red plastic monkeys on the floor.

The door opened and a lady came in, holding the hand of a little girl. The lady's stomach stuck out really far. It looked like hard work for her just to get to the counter. The little girl sucked her thumb. She stared at me. I picked up a monkey and started to make a chain by hooking one monkey's arm onto another's.

I had hooked seven monkeys when the little girl's feet appeared at the edge of my shrinking pile. "Me do," she said, holding out her hand. Her eyes shone black like two Apache Tears. That was a rock I'd read about the night before.

Mom came to the front and hugged the pregnant lady. As they started toward the back, the lady said something to her daughter in Spanish. I knew it was Spanish because that's what my friend Oscar's parents speak to him when we're at his house. The only word I understood was *Katie,* which I guessed was the girl's name.

I handed a monkey to Katie and dropped my chain on the ground so she had more to work with.

She picked up a monkey with the one in her hand, but when she got to monkey number three, the second one kept falling off. "Monkey *malo.* ¡*Malo!*" She threw them on the ground. *Malo* must mean something bad, because Katie didn't want to play with them anymore.

I made my monkey face by pushing out my ears

and crossing my eyes. She giggled. I stood up and galloped around the room. I made a monkey sound. *"Whoo-whoo-whoo."* It felt good to make someone laugh doing the thing that boy in the park had done to make me feel bad.

She laughed harder and clapped her hands. "Monkey *loco*." Then she chased me around the room.

She stopped in front of the toy box. She pulled out a tiny teacup and led me to one of the small chairs. She sipped from her cup and pointed to the one in front of me. I was glad none of the guys from Tae Kwon Do were here. I pretended to drink.

Fortunately, the girl's mom appeared before I had to pretend much more. *"Vámonos, Katita."*

Katie waved at me as they walked out the door.

"She's got the same name as you," I said to Mom after they were gone.

"Belinda liked the meaning,'" she murmured. She reached into her mailbox and pulled out a pink piece of paper. "Pure."

That was what Ed had called his minerals. *Pure* substances.

I went back to the reception area and sat in a real chair. I had just started to read in one of my rock books about how pearls are formed when the door opened and Belinda appeared. She was holding her stomach. "My water broke!" Katie grabbed at her mom, crying to be picked up.

I didn't know how water broke exactly, but I could tell what was happening. Her baby was about to be born. Whoa! Would it happen right here in Mom's office? I knew I was staring, but I couldn't help it. I'd never seen a baby get born.

"Denise, call 911," Mom said firmly, rushing toward the door. "Bren, take Katie, please." I stood there. I didn't really *want* to see a baby get born. "Bren!" She picked up Katie and dropped her into my arms. I sat her on my lap and held her fist. It was as hard as stone. She bawled so loud, it hurt my ears.

Mom helped Belinda to the back. Other women who worked there came out of their offices and rushed into Mom's office.

"Come on, Katie. It'll be all right." I sat her on the couch next to my backpack. I tried to get her interested in the monkeys again, but she kept crying. She started to scoot off the couch. "¡Mamá!"

I pulled her onto my lap and held her tight. "It's okay. Shhh." I wished Denise would come take Katie, but she was still talking to the 911 people.

The office became like a cage full of big lady birds flying and fluttering everywhere. In the middle of all that, an Asian man came in carrying two brown bags. He asked me if I knew who had ordered the food, since no one else seemed to notice him. I told him I had no idea, but I wished it had been me. My stomach felt like a big, empty cave.

He must have heard my stomach rumbling even over Katie's crying, because he dug into the bag and pulled out two fortune cookies. He handed one to each of us, then went to the counter, where Denise had hung up the phone.

Katie stopped crying. I tore open the wrapper and showed her how to crack the cookie and pull out the fortune. "'A surprise is on its way,'" I read out loud. "Hey, this one's for you! You're getting a surprise today. Will you get a baby brother or a baby sister?"

"Sis-ser," she said, reaching for the cookie. She crunched it between her teeth. Her face glistened from her tears and snot.

"I guess you'll know soon." I started to break the other cookie, but she wanted to do it, so I let her. I pulled out the little white slip. "'The one who forgives ends the argument.'" At first I thought it was a boring fortune. Then I thought of Mom and Ed DeBose. They were still fighting, even though they hadn't talked to each other for more than ten years. Someone needed to forgive, but who would do it first?

After a while, the paramedics came and wheeled Katie's mom away. Katie's grandma came and took Katie with her. When everything was quiet again, Mom and I sat in the kitchen and ate noodles and fried rice off paper plates. One of the ladies had offered it to us.

I placed the fortune about forgiving on the table. Maybe if Mom saw it, she would think about Ed, and maybe she would realize that she needed to forgive him for not letting her see her mom before she died.

"Katie really took to you." Mom put her hand on my arm. "You'd be a great big brother." When she lifted her arm, the fortune was stuck to her skin. "What's this?" She peeled it off and read it. If it made her think of Ed DeBose, she didn't show it. "That's a good one," she said, putting it back on the table.

I shoved it into my pocket. Maybe if I showed it to Ed DeBose, it would make him think about this forgiveness stuff.

I thought of Katie's mom and the baby getting born, even as we sat here and ate sweet-and-sour chicken. Thinking about what I'd seen that day made my stomach do flip-flops. I drank some of my root beer. "Are you ever going to have another baby?"

She sipped from her glass of water, then shook her head.

"Why not?"

"Well . . . when you were born, I almost died."

"You did?"

"Yep." She stuck her fork into the pile of noodles on her plate and twirled. "I've known since then that I can't have another one."

I chewed my food slowly. I had never thought much about having a brother or sister, other than that if they were all like Dori, I didn't really need one. I liked it with just my parents, Gladys, Grampa Clem and me.

But suddenly I felt sort of alone, like a moon orbiting a planet all by itself.

"I never said anything before because I didn't want you to think it had anything to do with you. It's just the way it happened."

"Was that before or after Grandma DeBose died?"

"A little before."

"And your dad still didn't let you see her?"

Mom's fork froze in midair. "What?"

My ears got hot. "Nothing."

"Who told you?"

"Don't blame Gladys. I asked. She didn't tell me anything, really."

She sighed and put her fork down. "Look, Bren, we'll talk about it." I looked up. "Soon. A little at a time. Okay?"

I nodded.

"It's just very hard for me to discuss. Do you understand?"

I shook my head. I didn't understand and I wasn't going to lie about that.

"Yeah, I don't think I would either if I were you."

The carrots and peas in my unfinished clump of fried rice looked like gems in a mound of dirt.

"What would you think if we adopted a little boy or girl into our family?" she asked.

"And a salamander?" I didn't need a little brother or sister, but I'd wanted a salamander all year.

"Let's talk about it. You know how much I like sala-manders." She smiled at me. Mom had had a pet lizard in college.

That weekend, Katie's mom called. Katie now had a little brother. Even though she'd wanted a sister, maybe after playing with me, having a brother didn't seem so bad.

CHAPTER 14

The next week, Mom arranged for me to stay at Khalfani's every day that she was at work, which was fine with me except for the fact that I didn't have a bike to ride.

On Monday, we swam in his pool and played Ninja Blast on his computer and his mom made us corndogs for lunch. Even Dori didn't seem so bad.

On Wednesday, I packed my *Book of Big Questions* in case I could convince Khalfani to help me do some research.

I'd added some questions recently, like why wouldn't Ed let Mom speak to Grandma DeBose after I was born—even though she'd almost died? And why didn't Mom want to tell me about it? And how come buffaloes didn't tip over? And why did some people's breath stink so bad?

But the question that gave me the Jitters worst of all was about what had happened at the rock club meeting. I still didn't understand. Why hadn't Ed told the group who I was? I couldn't help wondering a little bit, way down in the bottom of my brain, if Ed had been embarrassed to call me his grandson.

And even though I didn't want to believe it, the thought wouldn't go away, like a gnat that keeps dive-bombing your face no matter how many times you swat at it: *What if he was embarrassed because of my color?* I had been the only brown-skinned person there.

Maybe Ed had a problem with black people after all—or at least with admitting he was related to one. I didn't like this hypothesis. It wasn't the true scientific thing to do, but I couldn't help it: I shoved it out of my mind.

———

After we swam in his pool, Khal played a video game on his handheld while I got on the Internet and searched for more info about thunder eggs. I still wondered what made them so round.

Here is What I Found Out: Millions of years ago, gas pockets, like air bubbles, formed in lava flows. Over a very long time, water oozed through cracks in the hardened lava and left behind minerals that filled the gas pocket molds. These minerals became the thunder eggs. Because the gas pockets were round, thunder eggs are round.

I found an Internet article by a man who got interested in thunder eggs when he was ten years old, just like me. When he turned fifteen, he decided to go to Oregon because he'd heard that the thunder eggs in that state were so amazing. He hitchhiked and jumped trains for six hundred miles just to get there!

Would I ever do something like that? Would I ever get to dig thunder eggs?

I knew one person who could take me—Ed DeBose.

The questions surfaced again. Was he glad I was his grandson? Would he take me digging?

I would just call and ask him directly. It was the only way to know.

———

After lunch, I told Khalfani I wanted to phone Ed. But first I brought up the broken pick. "I don't know what to do about it," I said.

"Tell him you lost it."

"But I didn't."

"So tell him you broke it."

"I didn't do that, either."

"So tell him some big bully in the park broke it."

"Oh yeah." I guessed that didn't make it seem so bad.

I didn't have the green flyer with Ed's phone number on it, so we looked it up in the phone book.

When Ed answered, I said hello. He recognized my

voice, and I got tingly all over, like I imagined it might feel inside Gladys's water-massage machine.

"When're you coming over?" he asked. "Got another specimen for your collection."

I tried to ask him about going digging for thunder eggs, but my jaw felt stuck. "I don't know," I said.

"How about Friday?" he said. "I've got some hematite for you."

Hematite. I'd been wanting a sample for myself. I would ask him my question in person.

"So I'll see you then?" he asked.

"Okay." I hung up and turned to Khal. "I'm going back to his house. You've got to cover for me."

On Friday, Mom dropped me off at Khalfani's, as she had all week. My fingers were so sweaty, they slipped off the latch when I tried to get out of the car. Good thing I had on that deodorant, and that Mom hadn't asked me what we were planning to do today. I didn't want to have to break *yom chi* again. She told me she'd see me at two-thirty.

Khalfani let me in. Mrs. Jones and Dori were in the kitchen making pancakes. "We'll eat in a few minutes, boys," Mrs. Jones said.

"In a few minutes, boys." Dori was like a large parrot—with braids.

We ran upstairs and went over the plan. We would

ask if we could go to the library. Mrs. Jones never said no to that—she was a teacher. Then Khal would ride me to the bus stop on his bike. He would go to Frye's Electronics and play video games on their display consoles until 1:47, when my return bus would show up. Then we'd pedal back to his house, in plenty of time before Mom arrived.

If Mrs. Jones asked about lunch, we'd say we had money and that we'd go to Wendy's for ninety-nine-cent hamburgers.

We ate our pancakes and Mrs. Jones's fantastic fried plantains. Thankfully, Khalfani did all the talking. He could've fooled the latest and greatest polygraph machine. He was as cool as a frosted mug of root beer. I felt a little guilty knowing I was making him an accomplice, but then I remembered all the times he'd gotten me into trouble and it didn't bother me so much.

We took off on Khal's bike. I gripped the back of the seat and Khal stood to pedal. My backpack hung off my shoulders. We wobbled for the first few seconds, but I used my legs to help us balance and we were sailing in no time.

On the bus, I glanced at my watch a lot. If it took five minutes to walk from the bus stop to Ed's, I needed to make sure I left Ed's no later than 12:55 to catch my bus back.

I timed myself walking to Ed's. It actually only took

four minutes, but I would still leave by 12:55. Maybe 12:50, to play it safe.

The truck was standing in the driveway. I climbed the steps and rang the doorbell. The dog barked. I waited, but Ed didn't come. I rang the bell again. P.J. whined and pawed the door, but Ed still didn't come.

My heart beat harder in my chest. Would Ed leave the dog alone inside? The truck was here. Why wasn't he coming to the door?

I walked to the end of the porch and peered through the window just beyond the railing, but the green curtains were closed, solid as a wall of split pea soup.

What if he had fallen and couldn't get up? Or worse, what if he'd had a heart attack and was—I couldn't even think it. I saw Grampa Clem lying in his coffin. One day he was reclining in his armchair, joking with me about Gladys's cooking, and then—gone.

"You bring that magnifying glass?"

I jumped. Ed stood at the foot of the porch stairs holding a bag of groceries.

"You're not dead!" I forced back the hot liquid that had sprung to the surface of my eyes.

"Not as far as I know." He stepped onto the porch and opened the screen door. I rushed forward and held it for him.

"I just thought—when you didn't come to the door . . ."

"I do go out occasionally." He unlocked the door and

pushed it open. P.J.'s tail wagged hard as he wound around Ed's legs. "Okay, calm down, I'll get your bacon going in a minute." P.J. barked at me. "Yeah, he can have some, too." Ed led the way to the kitchen. "We like bacon around here."

"Is that why your house smells?"

Ed's eyes got small and his lips looked like a fissure in a rock. Then one side of his mouth turned up in a half smile and his forehead wasn't bunchy anymore and he laughed his sharp laugh, like a pick hitting a stone face. "Ha!"

I looked at his eyes to see what his soul might be doing while his mouth curved up in that smile. Grampa Clem said some people can smile on the outside while inside they're disliking you plenty—but I didn't see anything like that in Ed's eyes. In fact, his eyes looked like polished stones. The dullness from the first time I'd shown up at his house had been replaced by a sparkly shine.

He put bacon strips in a pan. "How about a fried egg sandwich?"

"My mom makes those."

"Who do you think taught her?"

I was still full from the pancakes and plantains, but I could eat a fried egg sandwich anytime, even thirty seconds after Thanksgiving dinner.

"Come on over." He pulled out a carton of eggs. "We'll do a geology lesson while we're at it."

A geology lesson! I stood next to him.

He held up an egg. "This is the Earth."

"The Earth is round."

"If you're going to be a scientist, you've got to remember one thing." He tapped my forehead with his finger, like a bird beak pecking on me. " 'Imagination is more important than knowledge.' Albert Einstein."

He knocked the egg on the edge of the frying pan. Small jagged lines appeared in the shell. "The Earth is like a cracked egg. It mostly holds together, but when the pieces move"—he hit the egg again and yellow goo started to ooze out—"magma escapes. When the magma hardens, it forms rock."

He split the shell with his thumbs. The clear liquid hit the pan and started to turn white. He did one more. I kept waiting for him to break the yellow part like my mom does so it would mix with the white, but he didn't. The yolk sat untouched, in a perfect yellow circle in the center of each egg.

Time to move forward with my experiment. "Why didn't you let my mom see Grandma DeBose after I was born?" If my hoped-for hypothesis was correct, Ed would now give me his good reason. I would ask him about hunting thunder eggs and the rock club meeting later.

He opened a wooden box on the counter. The door slid up like on a garage. He pulled out a bag of bread and put two pieces in his toaster. "Have you learned about tectonic theory yet?"

Wait. Keep observing. The reason could still come.

"Scientists think that all the continents used to be one big landmass. They call it Pangaea."

Why wasn't Ed answering my question?

"But the Earth's crust is in pieces, like the cracked egg, and the pieces are floating around. As the pieces moved, the continents got farther apart." Ed flipped the eggs. They sputtered and sizzled as if they were angry. "Continental drift," he said.

"Won't they run into each other again at some point?"

"Probably. But we'll be long gone by then. It took them forty-five hundred million years to get where they are now." He put two more pieces of bread in the toaster. "Whole oceans apart," he said under his breath.

After the toast was done, he spread mayonnaise on it and slid an egg onto one side of each sandwich. He put bacon on our plates and gave a piece to P.J. We sat at the table and ate in silence. I could hear Ed's sandwich rolling around his mouth, getting mixed with saliva. He swallowed.

"You ever heard the story of J. Robert Oppenheimer?" he asked.

I shook my head, chewing slowly. If Ed had a good reason, he sure wasn't making it very easy for me to find it out.

"J. Robert Oppenheimer designed the atomic bomb. Brilliant man. A true genius." He tore off a piece of bacon with his teeth. "When Oppenheimer was five, his father took him to Germany to meet his grandfather, and his grandfather gave him a collection of rocks."

My ears tuned in when I heard that.

"When the little boy returned to the United States, he kept learning about rocks. He even wrote to geologists at universities to ask them questions and tell them about his discoveries."

"I never thought of doing that," I said.

"Well, you still could. The boy's letters were so advanced, the geologists assumed he was an expert and they invited him to come speak at one of their meetings."

"How old was he?"

"Twelve."

That was only a little older than me! I chewed faster.

"When he showed up at their meeting, they were shocked, of course. He had to stand on a box to deliver his speech." Ed threw P.J. another piece of bacon. "What Oppenheimer liked about rocks were the crystals, their structure. How did rocks come to be as they were?" Ed looked at his plate as if he were examining *its* crystal structure. "How did things get this way?" His forehead looked like dry clay, full of deep cracks.

"Why did he make a bomb?" I asked. "Bombs kill people."

Ed's blue eyes looked cloudy again. "It's like I said before. People are complicated."

A knock came from the other room. I jumped in my chair. P.J. barked like crazy.

"Calm down, now. It's just the door." I wasn't sure if Ed's words were meant for P.J. or me, but I couldn't help my jumpiness. What if Mom had somehow found out? I stood in the kitchen and peeked around the wall.

A black man stepped inside. "I got a good feeling about today," he said, slapping his hands together.

"You say the same thing every week. And I win every time."

"Not true. There was that one time—February 16, 2001."

They both laughed. Why did the man keep coming back if he always lost? And what did he lose at?

He saw me then. "Well, hello there," he said. "I didn't realize Ed had company already."

"Hi," I said.

Ed looked over at me. "This is Brendan." He looked toward the man again. "My grandson."

My eyes widened at the same time the black man's narrowed. "Your grandson?"

An electric current traveled through my body. Ed had called me his grandson!

"This is Levi Henderson," Ed said. "We play chess every other Friday."

Mr. Henderson held out his hand and we shook.

"It's a pleasure to meet you, Ed's grandson." He turned to Ed. "I didn't know—"

"Enough stalling. The board is calling." Ed walked toward the chess set in front of the bookshelves. "You started last time."

"Oh, no. You're not pulling that one on me again."

"You did!"

"Brendan, would you tell your granddaddy here that he's going senile?"

"I'm sharp as cheddar cheese, and you started last time."

"Did you know your grandpa doesn't just collect fossils? He *is* one. Can't even remember what happened two weeks ago."

"Brendan, think of a number between one and ten," Ed said.

I picked three.

Mr. Henderson picked four and Ed picked five.

"It was three," I said. Ed grumbled. Mr. Henderson roared. They pulled up their chairs while I dragged one from the kitchen. P.J. plopped on the floor by Ed's feet.

Mr. Henderson sat on the side of the board with the white pieces. "Look who gets to be white!"

"Is being white better?" I asked. I didn't know anything about chess, but I was definitely looking forward to learning.

"Some people think so." He winked at me. I suddenly felt like I was sitting there with my two grandpas. Grampa Clem used to wink at me like that, too.

"White goes first," Mr. Henderson said. "That menas the White player always has an adventage."

"Not much of an advantage, if black plays it right," Ed said. "And I know how to play it right. Now, let's get this show on the road." His hands rubbing together sounded like sandpaper on wood.

Mr. Henderson moved one of the short white pieces in the front row forward.

Ed picked up a piece that looked like a horse head and jumped it over his front row.

"You don't have to move the front ones first?" I asked.

"I like to get my knights out fast, because as I always say—"

"'A knight on the rim is grim.'" Mr. Henderson finished Ed's sentence. "Your granddad hasn't taught you about chess?" He moved another piece.

My eyes flicked to Ed, then back to the board.

"The boy's into science—got my interest in minerals." Ed moved one of the short ones forward, then stood. "Speaking of which—" He left the room and came back.

He dropped a black chunk into my hand. "Here's your hematite."

I held the mineral between my fingers and twisted it around to see every side. This one looked different than Morgan's kidney ore. It had sharp edges instead of round ones and it sparkled.

Looking at the hematite made me think about the eeting. Now was my chance. "Why didn't you tell the eople at the rock club I was your grandson?"

Mr. Henderson glanced at me, then stared at Ed. He rossed his arms and raised one eyebrow.

Ed considered the board. He moved the piece that vore a pointy crown. "I guess I'm still getting used to the dea. You're my only one, you know."

I nodded. Uncle Chris didn't have any kids.

I wasn't sure what I thought about Ed's answer, but I didn't have time to think about it because my questions about chess started piling up. What was a rook and why did it look like the tower on a castle? Were some pieces more valuable than others? And how did Ed and Mr. Henderson know what piece to move when?

After a while, only a few pieces were left because every time one piece landed on another piece's square, the second piece was "captured" and taken off the board.

"Check and mate!" Ed hollered.

Mr. Henderson rubbed his cheek, scowling at the board.

Ed grinned. "So, you feeling like a glutton for punishment? Ready to go again?"

Mr. Henderson leaned forward and opened his eyes wide. "You're going *down*," he said.

After he won the second game, Ed brought us

lemonade and crackers with pineapple cream cheese spread on top to celebrate his victory.

Watching the third game, I secretly rooted for Mr. Henderson. And I tried to make sense of how Ed had responded to my questions. He hadn't answered my first one, and I wasn't sure if he'd answered the second. He was still hiding something; he wasn't practicing complete *yom chi*.

Mr. Henderson won this time, although Ed kept saying it was best two out of three, so he was still Overall Champion of the Day.

The whole time they played, I hadn't looked at my watch once or even thought about the bus. When I finally glanced at my wrist, I popped out of my chair and grabbed my bag from the kitchen. "I've got to go!" I yelled.

"Hold your horses. What's going on?" Ed asked.

"My mom's picking me up at two-thirty and I missed my bus!"

"Better give the boy a ride," Mr. Henderson said. "I'll close up shop."

Ed looked like he'd seen a ghost. "Uh . . ."

Mr. Henderson nudged Ed's shoulder. "What are you waiting for? You want the boy to get in trouble?"

Ed stumbled to the table under the picture of him and Grandma DeBose with Mom and Uncle Chris. He picked up his keys, then we got into the truck and sped toward Tacoma.

I had to take deep breaths the whole way to avoid losing my *guk gi*—self-control. Especially down below. The pancakes, egg sandwich and pineapple cream cheese had reached my large intestine.

I told Ed I needed to go to the bus stop, where Khalfani should be waiting. It was just 1:45.

As we got nearer, I could see Khal's round head. He was balancing on his bike, holding on to the pole.

Ed pulled up to the curb and I started to get out.

"Tell your friend to put his bike in the back. I'll drive you."

I glanced at my watch. We would make it in time on Khal's bike, but getting a ride seemed better. "Okay."

I opened the door.

"Man, you should have seen me playing NBA Slam 'N' Jam. I was awesome!" Khalfani said. "How come you're not on the bus?"

"Missed it." We got the bike into the truck and climbed back into the cab. Khal directed Ed to his house.

When we got there, Ed stopped across the street. I had been checking my watch the whole way. 2:04. Plenty of time. Hopefully Mrs. Jones wouldn't see us getting out of the truck. Khal hopped out and went to the back.

"Big place." Ed peered out his window.

"Thanks for the ride," I said, stepping onto the sidewalk. This was my chance. If I was going to ask, I had to do it now. "Could we go on an expedition sometime? For thunder eggs?"

The corners of Ed's lips pulled down. "Don't see why not."

"Great!" I thought for a moment. "How will I know when?"

"We'll figure something out." He hesitated. "But let's not tell your mom."

"I haven't told her anything." I swung the door shut and patted the side of the truck. The truck I had driven.

When I looked up, Mom's red car was zooming toward us. I started to duck, but she'd already seen me. Our eyes met.

It was too late.

CHAPTER 15

The brakes screeched. The door flew open. She stormed toward us. "What are you doing with him?"

I started to stutter an answer—I didn't know what, just something, anything—but she was glaring at Ed.

His window was open, but if he said anything, I couldn't hear it.

"Brendan, get in my car. Now."

"He didn't do anything," I said.

Mom turned her laser eyes on me. Her neck and face had turned bright pink. The Momometer was about to burst. "I'll be the judge of that. Now do what I said."

Khalfani stood near the back of the truck, looking scared. "See you later," he whispered, then jumped on his bike and zoomed across the street. He dropped the bike on the front lawn and slipped inside his house. I looked both ways about ten times and could have crossed ten times, too, but stalling is one of my secret skills.

"What is going on?" she yelled.

I thought I heard Ed say, "He found *me*, Kate," but I couldn't tell because the motor sounded like it was choking, and so did Ed. I shuffled toward Mom's car with my backpack over one shoulder.

"I don't care. Just stay away from him. You hear me?" Mom wasn't hard to hear. "*Stay away.*" She pounded her fist on the hood.

When I looked back, Ed had rolled up his window. He didn't look at me. He just drove off.

Mom fell into the car and slumped over the wheel. Her shoulders shook as if she was crying, but she didn't make any sound.

I've only seen my mom cry a few times—when she broke her ankle sliding into home plate at a police department picnic, when one of the pregnant girls she had helped killed herself and at Grampa Clem's funeral.

The seat and everything around me felt like sandstone, like if I spoke, the walls might crumble.

After what felt like a really long time but according to my watch was only two minutes, Mom sat up, wiped her nose with the back of her hand and got out of the car.

"Where are you going?" I asked.

"Same place as you. Get out."

She led me by the elbow to the front door and rang the bell. Khalfani's mom answered.

"Kate, you're early. Is something wrong?"

I kept my eyes down.

"Brendan, I believe you owe Mrs. Jones an explanation. And an apology."

"We didn't go to the library," I said quietly. I stared at the small stones that made up their porch. "Sorry."

"Then where did you go?" Mrs. Jones's voice stayed steady, calm. Then suddenly, "Khalfani!" She turned and looked toward the stairs.

"I went to see my grandpa," I said. "Khalfani just took me to the bus stop. He only did it because I asked him to."

"I'm so sorry about this, Doreen. Brendan will be punished, don't worry."

Mom was silent the whole way home. When we pulled into our driveway, she turned off the car and sat. "You're not seeing him anymore."

My face got hot. "What do you mean?"

"Exactly what I just said."

"Why not?"

"Because I said so. He's a mean man."

"You're the one who was mean."

Her head turned so quickly, I was surprised she didn't break her neck. "You don't even know the half of it."

"Because you won't tell me."

She put her hands over her face and exhaled loudly.

Her hands dropped in her lap. "I don't want you around him. And that's final."

My hands balled into fists. "You can't tell me what to do, because he's *my* grandpa!"

"Well, I'm your mother, and I still know what's best for you. That cranky old man in his run-down truck *doesn't*."

"I like his truck better than your stupid car." I almost said that he'd let me drive it, but I stopped myself just in time. "And *he's* a scientist. Like me!" I got out and slammed the door as hard as I could.

I was going with Ed on that expedition. Nothing would stop me now.

CHAPTER 16

I was grounded for two weeks. I couldn't go to Khalfani's. I couldn't even go beyond our front yard, except to attend Tae Kwon Do. Dad would call every hour when he and Mom were at work, and I had to answer the phone.

I spent Saturday morning in my room. A knock came at my door. I could tell it was Dad. He knocked like a police detective.

If it had been Mom, I might not have answered, but if I did that with Dad, I'd get into worse trouble than I already was in. "Come in," I said. I sat at my computer, reading on the Internet about caring for a pet salamander.

Dad sat on my bed. "You're old enough to know the truth," he said. "Your mom finally agrees with me."

The truth. What I'd been searching for all along.

What every scientist was after. What every Tae Kwon Do warrior defended.

I turned and faced Dad. He put his hands on his knees and looked me in the eyes. "Your grandfather didn't want us to get married because I'm black. When we did, he cut off ties with your mom and they haven't spoken since."

"But—" My insides felt like a sleeping bag stuffed into a small sack and cinched tight. I wanted to say, "He's been nice to me, he's given me his minerals, and he plays chess with Mr. Henderson." Those things didn't change the facts, but couldn't Ed have changed?

I slumped back in my chair, trying to make sense of this new data. Hard data that couldn't be denied.

Ed DeBose had been like those bullies in the park. Even if he was different now, at some point he hadn't thought black people were as good as white. The hypothesis I hadn't wanted to consider was the correct one after all.

"I don't get it" was all I could think of to say. I stared at the rocks in my window.

"You know what Tae Kwon Do teaches about parents."

"To respect them," I said. "But what about Mom and Ed?"

"For now you need to do what she has asked. No more visits behind our backs. She may come around eventually...if you still want to see him."

I glanced at Dad, pulled my lips to one side. Did I? I didn't know.

Dad patted my shoulder, then left the room.

I pulled out Ed's magnifying glass and held it over my arm. I looked at the black hairs growing like grass out of the tiny holes in my skin. I tried to see inside the holes to what was underneath. But all I could see was brown.

Brown. The color Dad had painted our house. The color of Mom's healthy pizza crust. And the root beer I loved to drink. And like Grampa Clem's skin, except lighter. Milk chocolate.

Or the color of dirt.

Ed had told me that without soil, we couldn't live. There'd be no trees and plants, no oxygen.

I looked at my skin again. If the brown on my skin had been dirt, I could have washed it away. Was that what Ed DeBose wanted? For us all to be the same color? Then would he have loved me enough to find me, instead of the other way around?

———

That night, Gladys came over so Mom and Dad could attend a police fund-raiser. If my parents had told her about my secret visits to Ed's, or about me getting into trouble, she didn't say anything, thankfully.

Sitting at the table eating Mom's pizza, I asked Gladys again why some white people thought black people weren't as good as them.

She pushed her glasses up on her face. "I used to ask myself that question all the time. Clem never did, but I did. And you know what I figured out?"

"What?"

"There is no explanation. So I stopped asking, and went on living. Just because someone can't appreciate beauty doesn't mean God's gonna stop making it." She put her hand on my arm. It felt rough against my skin. "Look at you."

I was brown, but I came from white people, too. A mixture. Like a rock more than a mineral.

Ed DeBose liked minerals better. Because they were *pure*.

After dinner, I went to my room. I opened my *Book of Big Questions*. Next to my question "What makes white people be mean to black people?" I wrote, "No answer."

Even as I wrote it, though, my palms itched and my stomach fizzed. I didn't like not having answers. Not having an answer was like Gladys not being able to figure out the last word on her crossword puzzle, or one of Dad's screwdrivers not being in its place. None of us could do anything else until that space was filled.

If I asked Ed DeBose this question, what would he say? Would *he* have an answer for me? I would ask him, straight out. As Grampa Clem would say, no more beating around the bush.

CHAPTER 17

At the police fund-raiser, Mom and Dad won a fancy overnight getaway at some expensive hotel. Gladys would spend the following Friday night and all day Saturday with me.

It was my chance. I would sneak away—one last time, I *promised*—and ask Ed for an explanation of what he'd done. I would be disobeying Mom, but I needed an answer to my question. And she wasn't going to let me see him—at least not for a very long time.

Plus, what if Ed had changed his mind about Mom and Dad's marriage but, like Gladys said, was just too stubborn to admit it? Maybe he knew things were broken and he just didn't know how to fix them, like me with the pick in my closet. But maybe I could help bring everyone back together again.

I also wouldn't mind having that thunder egg I wanted.

––––––––

On Monday, I called Ed. He didn't pick up, and no answering machine came on. I tried five more times that week before I finally reached him Thursday night. I had to whisper because my parents were home.

"Didn't think I'd be hearing from you again," he said.

"I've called you six times. You should get an answering machine."

"Don't need one," he said.

I didn't have time to argue. "This Saturday." I felt like one of the undercover detectives Dad works with. "Can we go on the expedition?"

The line buzzed between his phone and mine.

"I don't know about that, now. Your mom—"

"She's going away. It'll work."

"Well...I guess if you really want to go. It's hard for me to turn down a request to hunt thunder eggs. Six a.m. At the end of your street."

"Six a.m.," I repeated.

"Make sure you bring a hat. The sun can get hot."

"Okay. Um, Ed?" It was the first time I'd called him anything. He didn't respond. "Are you glad?"

"About what?" he asked.

"That I'm your grandson." I held my breath.

More silence. The buzzing sound moved into my head.

"Sure I am," he said.

My heart jumped into my throat.

"Saturday morning, then," he said.

"Saturday morning." The expedition was on.

Friday night, I told Gladys I didn't feel well so I could go to bed early. I even skipped ice cream to make it seem more convincing. She tried to get me to suck on the thermometer, but I talked my way out of it. I would feel better if I just went to sleep, I said.

In my room, I ripped a piece of paper out of one of my notebooks. I needed to write Gladys a note. I didn't want her to do something crazy like call the police, which she would do if I disappeared with no explanation. And if she did that, the police would contact Dad in a nanosecond.

I sat at my desk and wrote.

Dear Gladys,

You might be mad when you read this, but try not to be. You always say you like surprises, right? SURPRISE! I've gone on a rock expedition with Ed DeBose. I don't know if Mom and Dad told you, but I found out where he lives and I've gone to see him a few times.

Now I need to ask him about something very important.

*So don't worry, and if my mom calls, please don't tell her. I
don't mean to make you an accomplice, but this is just
something I have to do. If you help me out, I will buy you
one of your favorite Peanut Buster Parfaits at Dairy Queen
(even though there are way too many peanuts per square
inch in those things). I will be home before dark.*

Your Milk Chocolate,
Brendan Samuel Buckley

I folded the note and wrote Gladys's name on it.
Then I put my question notebook, my Tacoma Rainiers
cap and some money from my tackle box into my backpack and lay down to sleep. When I closed my eyes,
though, all my thoughts whirled around my head like
atoms.

I got up and put Ed's black bundle into my backpack—
broken pick and all. It was time for me to give it back to
him and tell him I was sorry I'd let it get busted.

Then I stretched out on my bed and waited for the
sun to rise.

———

When the alarm on my watch went off at 5:15, I shoved
my arm under my pillow to muffle the sound. A gang of
wild geese could probably land on Gladys's head and she
wouldn't wake up, but I didn't want to take any chances.

I brushed my teeth quietly, then grabbed my backpack and tiptoed into the kitchen to get a root beer. I

pulled on the fridge door and a bottle of salad dressing fell over, setting off a chain reaction. The crash sounded like a multicar pileup in the silence of our house.

I held my breath, waiting to hear Gladys's door open and her croaky voice asking me what I was doing up so early. I peeked around the corner. Nothing.

I grabbed a root beer, then decided to take two, one for Ed. I put my note to Gladys on the counter and slipped out the door into the early gray light.

When I got to the end of my street, my watch said 5:57 a.m. Ed had said you can't be too early. I watched for his truck to come over the hill. At 5:59, it appeared. My body felt like it was having an earthquake. I couldn't tell if I was cold or nervous or both.

What if Mom and Dad came home early? What if my note spontaneously combusted and Gladys didn't know where I'd gone? It could happen. I'd read stories about spontaneous combustion—where something, or someone, suddenly caught on fire for no apparent reason. I knew there must be a reason and science could explain it, but so far no one had figured it out.

The green truck pulled up to the curb. "You're on time," Ed said as I got in. P.J. barked from the back. He jumped up and put his front paws on the window between us. His breath steamed the glass.

"I have an alarm on my watch," I said. "It works underwater up to five hundred feet."

"That's handy. In case you ever need to meet someone at a sunken ship. You wouldn't want to be late to that."

I couldn't tell if he was being serious or making fun of me. We drove in silence. I looked out the window a lot. Was it okay just to be quiet? Grampa Clem and I were always quiet when we went fishing, but it didn't matter, because we were used to each other. Ed DeBose and I weren't so much.

Plus now I knew the secret about him, the reason I hadn't known him all these years. The truth hung in the air, unspoken. I could almost feel it, like a boulder sitting between us.

"Where are we going?" I asked.

"Red Top Mountain."

"Have you been there before?"

"A few times, but not to the place we're going. My buddy told me about a new spot."

We were silent again for a long time.

"Want a maple donut?" He pointed to a white bag on the floor by my feet. "Bought 'em fresh this morning."

I picked one out. The frosting oozed over my fingers. I bit into it and the sweet stickiness coated the top of my mouth and made my teeth shiver.

"Kind of gooey, but they're good," Ed said, taking a bite of his own.

I finished the donut and wiped my fingers on my

pants. My eyeballs felt coated with a thin layer of sand and my eyelids drooped in spite of how hard I tried to keep them open. I leaned my head against the door and fell asleep.

A bump to the side of my head woke me up. The truck was bouncing along a gravel road. Pine trees closed in on either side. The road grew narrower with each turn as we wound our way up a mountain.

"How long have we been driving?" I asked.

"Couple hours."

A couple of hours? I'd slept the whole way.

We came around a bend and Ed slowed down. I sucked in my breath.

Two gigantic animals, like horses with small heads, tiny ears and huge bodies, stood less than twenty yards away! Their reddish brown fur gleamed in the sunlight. They looked at us, then trotted up the road. Their rear ends were light tan.

"What do you think about that?" Ed asked.

"Are they moose?"

"No moose around here. Elk cows. Females. See how they don't have antlers?"

I nodded as the elk turned sharply and disappeared down the hill to our left. When the truck reached the spot where the elk had been, I looked into the young pine trees, standing side by side like rows of Roman soldiers. The animals had been so large and yet, just like that, they had vanished, as if they'd never been there at all.

"People go to London and Paris to see what they think are the wonders of the world, but I could stay right here and not see everything I want to before I die."

I didn't like Ed talking about dying, but at that moment, I felt exactly the same way.

The truck climbed and climbed until I thought we would drive into the bright blue sky; then the road flattened and we drove along a ridge. Across the valley rose mountains like the one we were on. Trees, everywhere I looked. The pointy green tips crowded so close together, I could have been seeing double. I squinted. A giant green blanket covered everything.

Ed pulled over at a wide spot in the road and we got out. "That's where we're going." He pointed down the hill. "I love thunder eggs—like Christmas presents. You never know what you're going to find inside."

He grabbed a huge pick from the back of the truck. It looked like the kind miners used. "Think you can manage this?" he asked.

"Sure," I said, rushing forward and taking it. P.J. nipped at the handle. Ed turned back to the truck for a shovel. The air smelled a lot better than it did in Tacoma, fresh and cold like ice water.

A dark slash in the sky made me look up. A brown hawk dipped one wing and circled right over us. I

pointed it out to Ed and we watched it together—
dipping, soaring, floating.

Then we crossed the road and started down the
hill.

Thunder eggs, here we come.

CHAPTER 18

Ed pointed to a fluorescent-orange ribbon tied to the top of a short pine. "My buddy put those up to mark the way," he said.

Without the ribbons, we would've been lost. I felt like Lewis and Clark. No path. Not even footprints. The brush came halfway to my knees and I had to pick my feet up high each time I stepped.

Bushes rustled nearby and my legs jumped to action, ready to perform a *yup cha gi*—side kick. Brown and white fur flashed between the trees.

P.J. I hadn't been able to see him through all the growth. I exhaled, then kept tromping through the brush.

I held the pick in front of me and used it to push tree limbs out of the way. Ed's jerky movements caused branches to whip around everywhere. I used *sang dan mahk kees*—high blocks—to keep from getting smacked in the face. Dew soaked my shirt and pants. We kept going down.

By now, Gladys had found my note. I could see her yelling at me, or more accurately, at the air. What if she called the police anyway? As long as I had my thunder egg and an answer from Ed by the time they found us, I didn't care.

My arms ached from holding the pick. Water drenched my face and shoulders. I kept my eyes on the back of Ed's heels. Step. Step. Step-step. I made a rhythm in my head. Step. Step. Step-Step. I got so focused on the rhythm, I didn't notice that Ed had stopped. My face crashed into his backpack. He stumbled forward. "Sorry," I said.

"Watch what you're doing, now. Don't want you to get hurt." Adults were always saying things about being careful and not getting hurt, but I didn't mind so much hearing it from Ed. Even though I knew what he'd done in the past, it was still nice to have a grandpa to go places with again.

We reached a clearing, a ledge with large rocks sticking out from the reddish brown dirt. The ground had already been dug up in places, including into the mountainside. Tree roots hung down in the cleared-out channels like pieces of used dental floss.

"This is it—where my buddy said there's a bed of

'em." Ed shook off his pack. "Been a lot of digging already." He took the large pick from me, raised it overhead and brought it down hard. I was glad Ed was going first. My arms felt weak after carrying the tool down the mountainside.

He grunted each time the end hit the ground. "You bring those tools I gave you?"

My throat tightened. "Yeah," I said quickly, my face hot. I waited for him to tell me to get them out, but he didn't.

After he had loosened the packed soil, he handed me the shovel. "Your turn," he said.

I could only get a small amount of dirt with each stab at the ground. This was going to take a long time. P.J. plopped onto the ground and looked at me with his head on his paws.

The end of my shovel clanged and P.J. sat up. Had I found one already? Ed bent over and picked up a dirt-covered chunk. Not an egg.

He brushed off the rock. *Phht.* He spit on it! He rubbed the place where his spit had landed. "Rhyolite," he said. "That's a good sign."

I smiled and dug faster, feeling like Popeye after a can of spinach. Each time my shovel disappeared into the dirt, I willed it to hit something solid. I imagined reaching down and pulling out the Thunder Egg that Ruled the World.

Digging for your own rocks took a lot more work than

just being handed them—but it felt a lot more exciting, too. I had wanted to become a rock hound this summer, and here I was, being one. This was the real deal.

I started slowing down again and Ed took over. I popped my root beer open and handed him the other can.

"Thanks." Ed stepped out of the hole we had created and sat on a rock. Should I ask him about what he'd done? Things were going so well. . . . I didn't want to ruin our good time.

He wiped his forehead with his handkerchief and chugged down what seemed like half the can before coming up for a breath. "Nectar of the gods."

Did God drink root beer? To me, God was a giant scientist, and the universe was His biggest experiment. "Do you believe in God?" I asked, leaning against a fallen tree trunk.

Ed blew his nose. "Can't say I think about that kind of thing all that much. I believe in what can be tested and measured—proven."

"My fifth-grade teacher, Mr. Hammond, says science can't prove. Only disprove."

"And God can't be proved *or* disproved."

I sat next to Ed on the ground. He had talked earlier about dying. "Where do you think we go when we die?" Mr. H. said this question couldn't be answered by science, but I believed it would be—one day.

"Back to the soil," Ed said, kicking up some dirt with his toe. A clod landed on my shoe. "In the end, we're all just dust." He raised his can to his mouth again.

There it was again. Dust. *To dust we shall return*. I crumbled the dirt clod between my fingers. Soil was broken-down rocks. Was Ed saying we were all just rocks?

But rocks didn't die. People did. I pictured Grampa Clem in his casket. "What about heaven?"

"Wishful thinking on the part of people who're afraid to kick the bucket."

I didn't like him saying that. Whenever I thought about Grampa Clem and where he was now, I imagined him on a boat reeling in a giant fish and shouting, "Ooo-ee, would you look at that one, Bren?" And I would think back to him, "Save some for me to catch." And he would say, "This is heaven, son. They never run out of fish here."

I looked at Ed. "If there's not a heaven, that means this is the only life we've got and when we die, it's all over. We're gone forever."

"That's what I believe."

My arms prickled. "If that's what you believe, why'd you let so many years go by without talking to us? That was a big waste of time." I hadn't planned it. It just popped out.

He squinted and his lips looked like that fissure

again, but he didn't say anything, just stared into the air. Then he got back in the hole and swung his pick as if the dirt had done him wrong.

I looked at his wrinkled face, leathery from the sun, red and sweaty from the hard work. Ed was old. He might not have that much time left. And if heaven didn't exist, I didn't have that much time left with him.

Finally, he stopped. He leaned on the pick handle, then stooped over and peered into a hole in the hillside. "Let's try in there. Hopefully whoever dug it left a few behind."

I stepped forward with the shovel, but Ed put out his arm. "I'll start." He took a smaller shovel from his backpack, then crawled into the shallow tunnel on his forearms. Only half his body would fit, though. His rear end and feet stuck out from the hill. I didn't know why he wouldn't let me do it. I would have fit a lot better in there. I heard the shovel stabbing the dirt at the back of the hole.

Stab, stab, clank, stab. "Did you find one?" I called.

"More rhyolite," Ed yelled back. He dug some more.

When it happened, there was no sound. The dirt above Ed's head fell in one big piece, like a giant rug covering him up. *Poof.*

"Ed!" I yelled, lunging for his feet. I could still see the bottom half of his body. P.J. barked wildly. I tugged on Ed's leg, but he kicked as if he wanted me to let go. He struggled to free himself, but it wasn't working. My eyes bounced around the landslide looking for a solution. How would I ever move all this dirt? Ed would run out of air first.

I heard his voice, muffled, but there. "Get help!" he called. Somehow he had room enough to yell. Maybe he'd be all right if I left.

But where would I get help? Not a single car had passed us on the road up the mountain. Only the elk. We were probably the only ones out here for miles. What should I do?

"Get help!" he cried again. P.J. barked and growled. He dug at the ground with his front paws.

I ran to Ed's pack and searched every pocket until I found his keys. If only he'd had a cell phone. But of course he wouldn't. He didn't even own an answering machine.

"I'm going!" I yelled. Then I sprinted up the hill, pushing tree branches out of my way and tripping over fallen logs. Limbs snapped under my feet. Twigs grabbed at my pant legs and poked at my eyes, but I kept moving, looking up and ahead for the orange plastic ribbons, flickering like flames against the Ellensburg Blue sky.

CHAPTER 19

It felt like forever until I found the truck. *In nae, in nae,* I said to myself over and over. Tenet number three. I would need perseverance to reach help in time.

Finally I saw the ridge where we'd parked. I ran as fast as I could the rest of the way. I put the key in the ignition and turned. The engine whined, then stopped. I wheezed, trying to catch my breath after racing up the obstacle-covered hill.

I tried the key again. Nothing. *What was I supposed to do now?*

Baekjul boolgool, I recited. Indomitable spirit. Courage in the face of adversity. I imagined Ed starting the truck. What did he do? Sometimes he put his foot on the gas as he turned the key. I tried it. The engine roared and the truck shook to life.

Keep your foot on the brake. Move the lever to D for drive. I needed to turn around. It would be a sharp turn, across the road, but this was an old logging road. No cars would be coming. I pressed down on the gas, turning the wheel hard to the left. The engine roared, but the truck stood still.

Emergency brake. My hand shook as I reached for the release. I pulled it and the truck started to move. I cranked the steering wheel left. I couldn't make it all the way around—at least not without going over the edge. I braked. I would have to back up and turn the wheel again.

Ed and I hadn't practiced going backward, but I knew that was what the R on the dashboard was for. I moved the lever and pushed the gas again. The truck zoomed back faster than I'd expected. I stomped on the brake and bit my tongue. "Ow." My mouth watered. My heart pummeled my ribs.

"Baekjul boolgool," I said out loud.

After a couple more tries, I got the truck pointed in the right direction. I gave it more gas. Too fast. Brake. Gas. Brake. The truck lurched down the mountain. *Baekjul boolgool. Baekjul boolgool.*

I got to the curvy part in the road. My knuckles ached from squeezing the steering wheel. My insides felt like they would fall out. I turned too far to the right and came dangerously close to the edge of the drop-off. I jerked the wheel left and the truck swerved toward the mountain.

"It's okay," I said, panting. It would be okay. Everything *had* to be okay. The road felt bumpier than before. Where was I going? How would I get help in time?

Ed would die. I knew it. After not knowing him my whole life, I had finally found him, and now he was gone, just like that. Just like Grampa Clem.

Hot tears burned the rims of my eyes. If I had stayed home like I was supposed to, this wouldn't be happening. Was this my punishment for not behaving like an honorable Tae Kwon Do warrior—for disrespecting my parents and being dishonest?

I worked to stay in the center of the road as I rounded the next curve, but my watery eyes made it hard to see. I blinked a few times.

A van!

I jerked the wheel to the left. Something hard jammed into my chest as the front of the truck crumpled against the side of the mountain.

———

The truck was silent. Pain. Around my heart. I couldn't breathe without it hurting. I'd forgotten to put on my seat belt.

"You okay?" someone yelled from outside.

"Huh," I said, because it was the only thing I could get out. I looked out my window, slowly, as if I were underwater.

A white man with a blue bandana on his head pulled open my door.

"Is he all right?" A woman with brown hair down to her elbows peered around his arm.

"I can't tell. Nearly killed us all, though. What are you doing driving, kid?"

"Who cares, Brian? Help him into our van." The woman stepped in front and took my arm. "Can you walk?"

"My grandpa," I said. My throat hurt from being so dry.

I told them what had happened; then we climbed into their van and started up the mountain. I sat on the shaggy carpet in the back, smelling gasoline and praying that God would help Ed stay alive, even if Ed didn't believe in Him.

———

Back at the digging site, P.J. clawed at the dirt. Ed's rear end was still up in the air—but he wasn't moving. Was he all right?

I ran to Ed. "Good dog," I said, pulling P.J. away.

Brian wrapped his arms around Ed's thighs. The woman, Tammy, grabbed one of his legs and I took the other. "Pull!" Brian said. I yanked as hard as I could. I fell backward as the hillside gave way and Ed popped out, red as a beet. He sat on the ground, gulping for air. His hair was full of dirt.

I was so relieved to see Ed alive that my chest stopped hurting. I thought about hugging him, but I was too embarrassed and he was all bent over, trying to catch his breath.

He coughed a few times. "I owe you one," he said to Brian and Tammy.

"Are you okay?" I asked, stuffing my hands into my pockets. It felt as if we were still in danger, standing there on that shifting mountain. The ground no longer seemed solid. The tunnel where Ed had been digging was gone.

Ed nodded. "Yeah. I'm okay." He held up a chunk of rock. "And I got this." He wiped it off and handed it to me. The rock was mostly black, rippled with blue. A *thunder egg!* "I think that's as good as we're going to do today," he said. He ruffled his hair and slapped at his shirt. Dirt flew everywhere.

"I can't believe you came out of that alive," Brian said. "How did you breathe under there?"

"A big tree root created an air pocket right where I needed it. Got lucky, I guess."

Was it just luck? I thought about my prayer in the back of the van.

"Like I said, I owe you." Ed looked at the place where he'd been buried.

"I'm just glad you're okay," Tammy said. My head bounced in agreement.

Ed gulped down some water, then offered me the

bottle. The water trickled cold all the way to my stomach. Then we climbed the hill and Brian drove us to Ed's truck. After making sure the engine would start, we thanked them again and said goodbye.

I leaned my head against the back window. The bone over my heart was hurting again, but I didn't care. We'd made it out alive.

"Sorry about your truck," I said. The fender had been pretty banged up and the left headlight was shattered.

"You saved my life."

Warm waves rippled over me. Ed saw what I'd done as saving his life?

"The truck can be fixed." He sniffed. "That was a close one, though. A little too close." He smiled at me with one side of his mouth. "Better buckle up."

By the time we reached the bottom of the mountain, my insides felt like a tumbler full of rocks getting polished. The maple donut and root beer swirled together in the beaker of my stomach. They were having a bad chemical reaction—with potentially dangerous gases.

We stopped at a gas station and I went to the bathroom. Then I figured I'd better call Gladys and let her know I was all right.

I dropped in two quarters and dialed my number. "Please deposit thirty more cents," a voice said. I put in a quarter and a nickel and waited for the ring.

It rang three times and the message came on. I

listened for the beep. "Gladys? Are you there? I'm calling to let you know—"

"Have you lost your mind?" Gladys was breathing hard, as if she'd been doing chair-obics before coming to the phone. "You better be on your way home. Your folks will have my head on a platter if you're not here when they get back."

I told her it would be a few hours but I'd be there in time.

Before I got home, I had a question to ask Ed. A Big Question.

Inside the truck, Ed held out a bag of sunflower seeds, already shelled. I poured some into my hand and crunched them between my teeth. Ed drove onto the road.

I looked out the window at the forest around us. My stomach was still tumbling. I licked the salt from the sunflower seeds off my palm. I looked out the window again.

"My birthday's August twelfth," I said.

"That right?"

"Maybe you could come to my party."

"Doubt your mom would be too happy about that."

I saw Mom hitting the hood of Ed's truck with her fist.

"Why didn't you want them to get married?" I kept my arms by my sides and waited.

Ed's eyes searched the dashboard as if he had X-ray vision and could see the engine through the gauges. He rubbed his nose. Then he pulled on his ear—one of the ears that stuck out like mine. "I guess I didn't much like the idea."

"Why not?"

He tugged on his ear some more. "Well, I guess it just didn't seem right... at the time. Races mixing like that." He glanced in the rearview mirror.

He had confirmed the truth.

"You mean you didn't want my mom to marry my dad because he's black." I looked at his pinkish face. My skin tingled, as if I were a big peach getting peeled. My heart sat at the center of me, turning hard as a pit. "But you play chess with Mr. Henderson every week."

"That's different than getting married." The truck sped along the straight road.

"Why is getting married different than being friends?"

His face turned even pinker. He sat as straight as the trees outside the window.

"You're too young... for all the details. I just think families should look alike. White people belong with other white people and black belong with black."

I thought about quartz. Purple, pink, brown, clear—it came in many colors, but all the colors belonged to the same family. "You still believe that?"

He glanced toward me, then looked back at the road.

"Is that the real reason you told your rock club I was just a boy from the mall?"

His eyes narrowed. "I tried to tell Kate, the children are the ones who suffer."

I leaned against the door with my chin in my hand. I thought of kids I'd seen suffering on TV—ads that showed children with dirty faces and their bones poking through their skin, kids who always had their fingers in their mouths and flies around their eyes. That wasn't me.

"I'm not suffering," I said.

We were silent the rest of the way home.

CHAPTER 20

Back at the end of my street, Ed pulled over to the curb. P.J. barked and scratched on the window.

Ed picked up the thunder egg from the floorboard and held it out. I took it in my hand, but all I could think about was that Ed didn't think we belonged together. I got out of the truck. I didn't care if thunder eggs *were* like Christmas presents. It sure didn't feel like Christmas.

I had hoped Ed would tell me something that showed he'd changed his mind—that he didn't think the same way anymore. I'd hoped he'd say how sorry he was and what a big mistake he'd made. But he'd given me nothing.

I gripped the rock. I wanted to hurl it at him. I felt like a big, angry thunder spirit.

I raised the thunder egg, ready to smash it to the ground. P.J. barked.

"Wait!" Ed said. "We need to *cut* it open."

I looked into his eyes. What I saw wasn't hate or dislike, the feelings that swirled around my heart like a hurricane. What was that word Gladys sometimes used to describe white people?

Ignorance.

Ed didn't have any idea why I'd wanted to throw the rock.

"You can keep it," I said, tossing it onto the seat. I zipped open my pack and pulled out Ed's tools. "I'm giving these back. Some boys in the park took the pick from me and broke it. They thought they were better than us, too." I dropped the black bundle on the seat. "I'll send you the money to replace it."

Ed stared at the tools.

I put my hand on the camper shell's window and P.J. licked the glass. "Bye, boy."

Was P.J. a brown dog with white spots, or a white dog with brown spots? Didn't matter. To me, brown and white looked like they belonged together just fine.

————

I tromped up my front steps and turned the doorknob. Locked. I started to reach into my backpack pocket for my key, but the door flew open.

Gladys grabbed my arm and pulled me inside. She

held me by my shoulders. Her nostrils flared and her breath was hot on my face. Then she pulled my head into her chest and squeezed.

"Sorry, Gladys," I said, and I truly was. Sorry that I had gone. Sorry that I'd met Ed DeBose. Sorry for how he felt about my parents getting married. For how he felt about me.

I pulled back. "Are you going to tell my parents?"

"No. But you are."

My hands were dirty. I went to the kitchen to wash them. I didn't want any reminder of my day with Ed DeBose. The experiment was over. I had my answer. But still no grandpa.

———

After my parents got home, Gladys raised her eyebrows a lot and kept poking me in the side when they weren't looking. When Mom and Dad went to put their suitcases away, I whispered, "I'll tell them tomorrow. Promise."

She crossed her arms and lowered her chin, but she didn't do any more poking or eyebrow-raising after that.

Gladys stayed for ice cream sundaes. While we sat around the table, Mom asked what we had done all day. I shoveled a huge spoonful of ice cream into my mouth so I couldn't talk.

"I'm sure Brendan will fill you in tomorrow. He's got lots to tell you." Gladys's mouth snapped shut. "As for me, I'm tireder than a petting zoo pony. Time for me to be getting home."

Dad left with Gladys. I said good night and went to my room. I sat at my desk, thinking. The rock tumbler that had been in my stomach earlier had moved to my head. My thoughts spun around and around. What scientific proof could be given to show that black people and white people shouldn't get married or have kids? The evidence actually proved the opposite.

Me. I was the evidence.

So what if one of my parents had brown skin and the other had white? It didn't make a bit of difference to the molecules that came together to make me. I'd learned in Mr. Hammond's class that I had some genes from my mom and some from my dad. Some genes from Grampa Clem and Gladys, and some from my mom's parents.

I had Ed DeBose's ears. He'd said so himself. And our interest in science—that could be genetic, too. It was possible.

He was my grandpa. We were blood-related, whether he liked it or not.

Didn't Ed DeBose know that science was supposed to be unprejudiced? I wanted to hit something, but I couldn't make noise.

I stood in front of the long mirror on my closet. I kicked to the front and my mirror self kicked back. I punched to the front. My mirror self punched back. Faster and faster, I kicked and punched. To the front.

The back. Left. Right. Finally one giant jumping kick, then I crumpled on the ground. I had nothing left to kick or punch. I had kicked and punched all my mad feelings out. I lay there, nothing moving except my lungs. No sound except my breath. Eyes closed. Darkness. And then against the black screen in my head, one tiny yellow word: *Why?*

One little word, only three letters long, but it was the biggest question I had ever come across. And science couldn't answer it.

CHAPTER 21

Sunday came and went (thankfully Gladys wanted to stay home because she'd been to our house Friday and Saturday), then Monday. Still, I couldn't seem to get the words out of my mouth that I'd gone with Ed on the expedition. Every time my parents came around, my tongue turned to cement. I kept telling myself I'd already been grounded for two weeks—how much worse could it get?

My birthday was coming up. What if they said I couldn't have a party—or there'd be no presents? I couldn't tell them.

Tuesday night was my purple belt exam. I spent most of the day in the basement, going over my forms. Mom and Dad came with me to the *dojang*. They sat in the back next to Khalfani's dad.

"How's prison life?" Khal whispered when I joined him on the mat. I hadn't even told Khal that I'd gone with Ed DeBose to hunt thunder eggs, but he knew that I'd been grounded for going to see him before.

"All right," I said, then fixed my eyes to the front, where Master Rickman was introducing the first testers—little guys who couldn't have been older than five or six. The *cho bo ja*—beginners—wore white belts symbolizing innocence. A very long time ago, or so it seemed now, that had been me.

We had to sit cross-legged and watch all the groups before us: white, yellow and blue. Just when I thought my butt couldn't take any more, Master Rickman called for the blue belts with purple stripes. Khal nudged me. We walked to the front.

Khal and I went first. I bowed, then stood in ready position. Each form we'd mastered required us to demonstrate a series of kicks and punches, in the correct order. Master Rickman gave us the signal, and we started to move through the *hyungs* for each level.

Chon-ji came so easily at this point that I didn't even have to think about it. Just like riding my bike.

My bike. Would I ever get it back? My parents were letting me earn extra allowance by doing more chores so I could buy a new one, which I'd do after I sent Ed money for the pick.

I forgot where I was in the sequence. I hesitated, feeling my ears get warm. I glanced at Khalfani, trying to remember what to do next, then jerked back into motion, hoping my mistake hadn't been too noticeable.

We moved on to *dan-gun*—planting the seeds. Then we were sprouting—*do-san*—the form for the yellow belt. Then on to *won-hyo* and *yol-guk*.

Finally I reached *joong-gun*, the pattern I'd learned after I received the purple stripe on my blue belt. I flowed through it like the water in the stream at Olympic View Park. It was a cinch.

After that, Khalfani and I had to demonstrate our kicks and punches in a sparring match. The hardest part was not touching each other. Our school of Tae Kwon Do uses noncontact sparring as a way to promote discipline. I spun, jumped and kicked. I blocked every one of Khal's punches. I finished with the "killing blow"—my fist an inch away from Khalfani's head.

The last thing we had to do was pass the *kyepka*—the break test. Master Rickman placed a board in the holder on the wall. Khal turned to the side, balanced himself and shot his leg through the wood. *Snap!* He'd gotten it in one try!

I wanted to high-five him, but I kept my cool.

It was my turn. I stepped into position and focused on the board. Just as I was about to raise my leg, I caught Dad's eye in the mirror. Suddenly I felt like Superman in front of kryptonite. I kicked in a feeble attempt, but I knew: I didn't deserve the purple belt.

Master Rickman let me try two more times. I broke the board on the third attempt, but still I knew. I couldn't take the belt, even if it was offered.

I bowed and returned to my seat on the ground. "What happened?" Khal asked. I just shrugged. The room was crowded and hot, the floor as hard as brick. My *do bok* seemed to have shrunk on my body. It felt two sizes too small. The belt was suddenly too tight.

By the time the brown belts got up to test, I wanted to run out of the room. At the end of this exam, Master Rickman would call my name, bow to me and present me with my new belt. A belt I couldn't accept.

I hadn't been noble at all. I'd snuck out of my house, almost gotten Ed killed, and then not told my parents what I'd done.

I'd found a way to feel okay about it before, but now, about to be honored as a purple-belt Tae Kwon Do warrior, I knew I was wrong.

I held myself still, feeling like a melting candle as sweat dripped down my face and sides. My deodorant was failing me big-time.

When Master Rickman invited me forward, I bowed, then stepped close and whispered in his ear. He put the belt back on the table and I returned to my seat, seeing my parents' confused stares.

When I went over to my parents afterward, I kept my head down.

"What was that all about?" Dad asked.

"I went with Ed again. To look for rocks." I held still, waiting for Mom to tell me what big trouble I was in, but she didn't say anything. "And because I needed to ask him for the truth. About what happened in the past. Because that's what scientists do. They search for the truth." I looked at them. "And Tae Kwon Do warriors are supposed to tell the truth. I'm sorry I wasn't honest."

"That's why you didn't accept your belt?" Mom asked.

"Purple stands for noble." I lowered my chin again, feeling my eyes get watery.

Mom pulled me into her arms. "Oh, Boo, sometimes people do things and don't know why. I guess it's time we talked about Ed."

I looked up at Dad. "Are you mad?"

"I think I can understand why you did what you did."

"Are you mad at Ed?"

"I was mad. But in the end it was his problem." He put his hand on my back.

"Science is supposed to be unprejudiced," I said, "but I guess that doesn't mean scientists always will be." Mom squeezed me again.

Dad patted my shoulder. "Your color is not who you are. Understand?"

I pulled back from Mom. *The streak test.* Hematite

was black, but its streak was red. "Color is just a part of who you are...like a mineral," I said. I remembered what that boy had said at the park, and the truth that everyone bleeds red. That was sort of like hematite, too, and like me. Black on the outside, red on the inside.

Dad rubbed my back. "An important part, but only a part."

Mom swiped my sweaty hair away from my face. "Now go get your belt," she said. "You've told the truth."

Back home, Dad went to the kitchen to make his specialty, macaroni and cheese, in celebration of my purple belt. I grabbed my *Book of Big Questions*. Mom and I were finally talking about Ed, and I had plenty to ask. Had Ed met Dad before he decided he didn't like him? Had he ever asked to meet me? Why did he think the way he did about blacks and whites getting married?

I wanted to know the real deal about Ed. It didn't make sense to keep the truth covered up. It'd been covered up all these years, and that hadn't helped anything. I would dig for answers as if I were back on that mountain looking for a thunder egg. And I would accept what I heard, even if it felt like taking an *ap cha gee*—front kick—to the gut.

Mom put her feet up on the coffee table. She patted

the couch next to her. "What's that?" she asked, pointing to my notebook.

"Brendan Buckley's Book of Big Questions About Life, the Universe and Everything in It." I sank onto the brown leather.

"Life and the universe, huh? Those *would* be some big questions." She rested her head on the back of the couch. "So, what kinds of questions does my curious kid have?"

I opened my book. "Well, for one, what makes bananas taste so good and peas taste so gross?"

"I'd be very interested to know what you find out about that." Mom doesn't like peas, either. "I guess you've probably got a few about your grandpa in there."

I nodded, scanning my list. Over the past couple of months, I had written down more questions about Ed than anything else. "Did Grandpa DeBose even meet Dad before he said you couldn't marry him?"

Mom shook her head.

I'd had a feeling that was the answer I'd get.

"They met the day we got married." She pushed herself up and put her feet on the floor.

"Ed was at your wedding?" It still felt weird to call him Grandpa.

"Not exactly. I told my parents your dad and I were getting married at City Hall, and they were welcome to come if they wanted. My father came—to stop us. He and your dad"—she hesitated—"exchanged some words."

Ed and Dad had had it out? *Whoa.* "Were Gladys and Grampa Clem there?"

She nodded.

That was how Gladys had known what Ed looked like. Apparently, Ed hadn't remembered *her* as clearly.

Mom continued. "Gladys wasn't exactly excited about your dad and me, either, but Grampa Clem helped her see that it would be all right. They stood by us when we said our vows, and from that day forward, they treated me like their own daughter."

"You said Ed knew about me. How?" The question wasn't in my notebook, but it would be soon, along with the answer.

"I sent my parents a letter after you were born. I guess I just wanted them to know."

I stared at my notebook. "Why didn't you take me to see them?"

She gazed in the direction of the chandelier over the table. "I was angry, and hurt. . . ."

"Did Ed ever ask to meet me?"

Mom looked at her feet. "He did."

"But you wouldn't let him?"

"I was angry, and hurt. Maybe keeping you from my father was my way to get back at him." She put her hand on mine. "I never meant to hurt you, sweetie."

I felt like one of Ed's chess pieces. Mom had used me like a pawn, trying to win the game. In the end, no one had won anything. We had all lost out.

"Did you *try* to make up with him?" I asked.

"As far as I was concerned, it was his responsibility to make up with me. He was the one who caused the problem. He needed to be the one to fix it."

I remembered the fortune I'd gotten at Mom's office. I still had it in my desk drawer. "The one who forgives ends the argument," I said.

Mom's eyelids lowered. She smiled. "When did you get so grown-up?"

"I'm almost eleven, you know."

She sighed. "I know."

"And that stuff about forgiveness is from a fortune cookie. Remember?" I grinned.

Dad poked his head out from the kitchen. "Grub's on in five."

I inhaled the smell of buttery cheesiness. *Mmmmm.* "So are you going to talk to him?" I asked.

Mom wrapped her arms around her middle as if she'd been cut in half and needed to hold herself together. "I'm not sure. Would you like me to?"

There was that question again. Did I want to see Ed anymore? I shrugged. "It was kind of nice having a grandpa again."

Mom nodded.

"But I wish I understood why he didn't want you to marry Dad, especially when he didn't even know him."

"That's a big question, sweetie. And the answer is even bigger. But what you just said gets at part of it.

People get caught up in appearances. We don't look beyond to the person inside."

I thought again about what minerals had taught me. A mineral's color was important, but it was only part of what made it what it was. The color on the inside— what you learned by scraping the mineral against a hard surface—told you much more about what that mineral actually was.

Mom put her arms around me and I let her hug me as long as she wanted, even if I *was* almost eleven.

CHAPTER 22

A couple of Sundays later, Gladys came over for dinner as usual. She had just asked what we were going to do at my birthday party when the doorbell rang. Mom pushed back her chair. "You expecting someone?" she asked Dad.

"Nope." He shook his head.

I sawed on my chicken. For my birthday the following Saturday, I'd invited Khalfani, Oscar and Marcus over for a pizza party, and I couldn't wait. I hoped my parents would get me the salamander I'd asked for.

The door opened at the bottom of the stairs, but no one spoke. I stopped chewing so I could hear.

"Who is it, Kate?" Dad called out.

Mom didn't reply.

"I—" A rough voice, like granite. I pushed out of my

chair and rushed to the top of the stairs. Ed stood at the door. His mouth made a straight line like a zipped-up zipper. The wrinkles on his forehead were dark lines. He glanced at me, then back at Mom. "I came to give Brendan something." He held a box wrapped in newspaper comics. An envelope poked out from underneath.

Mom stood in the doorway like a small giant guarding a castle. She didn't move. "This is quite a surprise," she said.

"For me, too." He shifted on his feet.

"Are you going to come in?" I asked. It seemed dumb for them just to stand there staring at each other. Plus I wanted to know what was in the package.

Dad's hand pressed down on my shoulder. Gladys came to my other side. "It's about time," she said under her breath, but loud enough that everyone probably heard.

Mom stepped back and motioned for Ed to come in. He stood in the corner while she closed the door, then followed her up the stairs.

"Ed," Dad said.

Ed nodded at him. At the top of the stairs, he handed me the box and card. "Happy birthday," he said.

"You remembered." I stared at the present.

Dad pointed to the love seat and Ed perched on the edge. His face was as pink as rhodochrosite. He wrung his hands between his knees. Gladys leaned back in the rocker, and Mom and Dad sat on the couch.

I shuffled toward the love seat. Sitting next to Ed reminded me of being in his truck. I set the envelope on the seat next to me and ripped the paper from the box. "My first birthday present," I said. "Just five days"—I looked at my watch—"four hours and fifty-two minutes until I'm eleven."

Ed chuckled.

I held up a wooden box with a glass lid.

"I made the box," he said, "but the real gift is inside."

I looked through the glass. Two sides of a cut-open rock sat in a cloud of cotton. It looked like a small brain sliced open to show the insides. One half was almost a mirror image of the other, but not quite.

I opened the lid and picked up one half of the rock. I turned it over in my hand. "It's the thunder egg we got!" I held it up for Mom, Dad and Gladys to see. "They know," I said to Ed. "That we went, I mean."

"Oh." He kept his eyes on the rock. "Actually, it's not a thunder egg."

My shoulders slumped. "It's not?"

"It's agate. The rare Ellensburg Blue. Probably worth a couple hundred bucks."

"Whoa," Dad said.

Two hundred dollars? I'd never had that much money before, but I knew I would never sell this beauty—not even for a new bike.

I set it back in its place. Sitting next to each other,

the two halves looked almost like a heart. In the center of the heart, black speckles like lead shavings made the shape of a cow's head. A clump of pinkish white crystals grew in a hole on the left side. Bluish stone filled in the rest, sometimes dark, sometimes light, like ocean water surrounding and connecting everything it touched.

"It's much better than the solid chunk I've got at home," Ed said. "I think the mix of black moss agate and white quartz with the blue makes it even more special." He winked at me. "What do you think?"

I picked up one of the halves and handed it to him. "I think you should keep half and I should keep half."

He put his arm around me and patted my shoulder. "No, no, this one's yours. I bet we can find us some more, though." I glanced at Mom. Her lips looked like a shut-tight oyster. Ed spoke again. "Did you know the only other place where rock like the Ellensburg Blue has been found is in Africa?"

I shook my head.

"Not surprising," Gladys said. "It's a land of greatness."

Mom crossed her arms. "What if something had happened to him? We would have had no idea where he was." If only she knew how close we'd come to something bad happening. I hadn't told her that part.

"You're right," Ed said. "It was irresponsible of me. Hopefully in the future we'll go with your approval." He looked at Dad. "And yours, too, of course. You've got one heck of a son."

"Yes, we do," Dad said.

"He's a heck of a grandson, too," Gladys chimed in.

Mom exhaled loudly, but at least she hadn't said we could never go digging together. Seeing Ed and the rock we'd found, I knew I'd want to go with him again. "Don't forget the card, Bren," Mom said.

I tore open the envelope. On the front, a stork carried a baby by a blanket in its beak. WELCOME, BABY BOY, it said. I felt my forehead wrinkle. A baby card?

I opened it. It was signed "Love, Grandma."

"Your grandma never had a chance..." Ed looked at his hands. "She loved you very much, even though she never met you." He cleared his throat.

I stood and handed the card to Mom. When she opened it, she sucked in her breath. Her eyes watered.

"I have something to share with you, too." I ran to my room, set the box on my bed and opened my desk drawer. I pulled out the library book I'd been reading the night before. My eye landed on the fortune from Mom's office. "The one who forgives ends the argument." I'd only applied it to Mom and Ed, but suddenly I realized it could also apply to me.

Back in the living room, I flipped pages, scanning

the words. I felt everyone's eyes on me. Finally, I found the sentence I was looking for. I read it out loud. "'Rocks, as with most other things in nature, are seldom exactly one thing or the other...granite and basalt in varying amounts make up a group of other rocks with in-between colors....'"

I closed the book and stared at the cover. It was called *City Rocks, City Blocks and the Moon*. I'd picked it because of the "moon" part. I still hoped to figure out how to get a moon rock of my own.

"I'm an in-between color," I said, "and I belong to both." Dad, Mom, Gladys—and Ed DeBose. "Both black and white people."

I looked Ed in the eye. "And I forgive you for what you did. And what you thought."

Mom made a sound like air rushing out of a balloon.

Ed stared at the carpet, his elbows on his knees.

"I was wrong, Kate," he said, finally, looking up at her. "I shouldn't have kept you from your mother. Sam, I'm sorry for how I treated you, as well." Then he gazed at me. His azurite-colored eyes looked like overflowing pools. Tears spilled out and ran down both cheeks like streams trickling down a mountainside.

"And you," he said, "I missed seeing you grow up." He pulled his handkerchief from his pocket and wiped his eyes and nose. "What a fool I've been."

I sank onto the love seat. "I'm not *all* grown up," I said, and then I was hugging him, smelling his clothes that smelled just like Mom's clean laundry. "Grandpa..." I said it quietly, but I knew he heard me, because he squeezed back.

"Mom?" I asked. "Can he have dinner with us?"

Mom glanced at Dad. He nodded. She blew air out of her nose. "Would you like to join us?" She motioned toward the table.

Ed stuffed his handkerchief into his back pocket. "Well...I mean, are you sure?"

My heart beat like a hummingbird's.

"I guess, well, if you're offering," Ed said. "I've never been one to turn down a good meal."

Mom warmed up the food while Dad found a chair and set it next to mine. I got out an extra plate and silverware.

"So Brendan tells me detectives and geologists are a lot alike," I heard Dad say.

Gladys poured Ed some of her Mountain Dew. "Your daughter only buys sugar-free," she said as she headed to the table. "Better get used to it."

Then we all sat down and ate together.

———

Later, in bed, I opened my *Book of Big Questions*. I read again the question I hadn't been able to answer: "What makes white people be mean to black people?"

I didn't think I knew the full answer, but it seemed to

me that in Grandpa DeBose's case, at least, it'd had something to do with a bad kind of pride, and maybe fear. Fear of what was different and of things he didn't know about. I was glad that when I didn't know something, I tried to learn more about it.

Like with dust and wondering where it came from. I remembered what I had learned. People create dust. And in a way, people *are* dust. We all eventually die—at least a part of us does. Maybe it was that dusty part that caused us to be mean and not very accepting at times.

But people could also change. Grandpa DeBose had changed.

I flipped back a couple of pages and found the reason I had opened the book in the first place. I checked off the question "What am I?"

Here is What I Found Out: I am a scientist, a mineral collector, a sometimes noble Tae Kwon Do warrior, a friend, a son, a grandson, someone who belongs to both black and white people, a mixture like a rock, my color but, much more, myself—Brendan Samuel Buckley.

Some More Things I Found Out About Rocks and Minerals

By Brendan S. Buckley

- Up to 100,000 tons of rock fall to Earth from space each year! The largest meteorite in the world lies in the ground in Africa and weighs more than 60 tons.
- A lot of dust is finely ground rock and mineral particles. Sixty percent of the earth's airborne dust comes from Africa's Sahara Desert, and some of it even reaches the U.S. The soil in my backyard might contain grains of dust from halfway around the world!
- More than 3500 different minerals have been discovered, but fewer than twelve minerals make up 97 percent of all rocks.
- Humans can't make minerals. And minerals are not alive. They are not plants or animals.
- Each mineral has one kind of molecule repeated over and over in a pattern (which is another reason Grandpa DeBose likes them—they're orderly).

- We use and even *eat* minerals every day: Pencil lead is the mineral graphite; table salt is halite; school chalk is gypsum; the little white *M* on M&M candies is made of two minerals, rutile and ilmenite, which also turn toothpaste and paint white. And they are in the white filling of Oreos.
- Muscovite is used to make glitter and to decorate Christmas trees with fake snow.
- Quartz (number 7 on the Mohs Scale of Mineral Hardness) is used in sandpaper, soap, radios, watches, TVs and computers.
- Sulfur is used in matches, fireworks and medicine.
- Without bauxite, we wouldn't have soft drink cans or aluminum bats.
- An ounce of gold can be hammered thin enough to cover a football field, or rolled into a wire long enough to stretch 50 miles.
- If you strike the mineral pyrite against flint or iron, it produces sparks. For centuries, people used pyrite to make fire. Pyrite is also called fool's gold because it sparkles like gold.
- President Abraham Lincoln was a rock hound, too. A museum in Iowa has a cigar box marked "Collection of rocks made by A. Lincoln" with his signature on the lid.
- The largest rock and mineral collection is in the Natural History Museum in London. It has 350,000 minerals and 100,000 rocks! I sure hope I can go there one day.

If you'd like to become a rock hound like me, you can call, write or visit your state capital, where there's a department called the U.S. Geological Survey (it's sometimes called a Natural History Survey or Bureau of Mines, depending on the state). This office can give you a map of rock and mineral collecting sites in your state. You can also write to or visit the geology department of your local college or university for more information.

And here's a great Web site for kids who are interested in rocks and minerals: http://library.thinkquest.org/J002289/index.html.

I hope you like collecting and learning about rocks and minerals as much as I do!

Some Interesting Facts About Tae Kwon Do

By Brendan S. Buckley

- In case you don't know, Tae Kwon Do is pronounced "tie kwon dough."
- Tae Kwon Do is a martial art form that started in Korea more than a thousand years ago, although it wasn't called Tae Kwon Do until 1950.
- It is especially known for its fast, high and spinning kicks (which is what I like most about it).
- In Korean, *Tae Kwon Do* means "the way of hand and foot," or "the art of kicking and punching."
- Becoming a black belt will probably take you two to five years, if you train two to three times a week. (I've been doing Tae Kwon Do for two years, and I hope to earn my black belt in one more year.)
- Tae Kwon Do became an Olympic sport in 2000.

- The first Tae Kwon Do students were soldiers and police officers (like my dad).
- Tae Kwon Do teaches you to respect your elders, family, friends and teachers, and never to take another life unjustly. You should also always finish what you start—which is why I had to find out the truth about Grandpa DeBose, but I learned that I shouldn't have disobeyed my parents to do it.
- The forms (or *hyungs*) that we practice in Tae Kwon Do are patterns of defending and attacking movements performed against imaginary opponents. Each level has a different form that you have to memorize and master before you can get your next belt.
- The first form, called *chon-ji*, means "heaven and earth" and represents the creation of the world, or the very beginning. That's why you learn it first.
- The second form, called *dan-gun*, is named after the man who founded Korea in 2333 BC, although Master Rickman says he's more of a legend than a real person.
- In the break test (or *kyepka*), you use your foot, hand, elbow, knee or head to break a wooden board, although some people also break bricks, tiles and even baseball bats! We do the *kyepka* because it requires concentration, focus, speed and accuracy. It's also a good way to learn that our bodies are strong weapons and we should be careful when we're sparring with our partner!

ACKNOWLEDGMENTS

I am eternally indebted to the many people who've encouraged me to pursue the significant calling of being a writer, starting with my parents, who've believed in me beyond what I've given them credit for. To author Kevin McColley and my advisors at Vermont College, Jane Resh Thomas, Louise Hawes and Sharon Darrow: The pieces of stories you helped me to write didn't end up in this book, but they got me to this point and hopefully will appear in others! To Norma Fox Mazer and Marion Dane Bauer, thank you for sharing so generously the invaluable gift of your experience. To my writing buddies, Nicole Schreiber, Lisa Bose and Joelle Ziemian, and my best buddy, Fina Arnold, as well as my current writers' group, thanks for reading various versions of this work, for the many fine ideas and insights and for cheering me on along the way.

A huge heartfelt thank-you to the best mentor anyone could wish for, Carolyn Coman, for giving so much. You prompted me to dig deep and find the dedication to make big changes, the discipline to value little details, and the determination to listen for my true voice. I greatly appreciate my agent, Regina Brooks, for her enthusiasm about my work and her zeal in everything she undertakes, and my editor, Michelle Poploff, for vitalizing Brendan's story with her kid-friendly vision.

On a practical note, thank you to fifth-degree black belt

Josh Henkel for checking my portrayal of Tae Kwon Do, and to Ed Lehman of the Washington State Mineral Council, who led me on my first rock expedition as I researched this book, and who, in one of those fantastic coincidences that occur when you write a novel, just happened to share Brendan's grandpa's first name.

Above all, much love and gratitude to my husband, Matt, for asking two of the Biggest Questions I'll ever be asked in my life, and to my daughter, Skye, for waiting to come until Mommy could finish this book. I love living my story with the two of you.

ABOUT THE AUTHOR

Sundee T. Frazier says: "When I first wrote this book, Brendan's grandpa didn't show up until the very end. Little did I know that the discovery of Grandpa DeBose was actually where Brendan's story began...but as Brendan says about asking questions, writing often leads to surprises, and it *always* leads to asking more questions."

Like Brendan Buckley, Sundee T. Frazier is proud to come from both black and white people. She is the author of *Check All That Apply: Finding Wholeness as a Multiracial Person,* and she especially wants to see young people grow up feeling good about their heritage and identities. Raised in Washington State, where she currently lives and has hunted for rocks and minerals of her own, she's also lived in California, Pennsylvania, and Wisconsin, and she completed her MFA in writing for children and young adults at Vermont College. She lives in the Seattle area with her husband and their daughter, and you can read more about her published work at www.sundeefrazier.com. This is her first book for children.

SALEM-PANOLA